YA W/D
Lev

Levin, Betty- The Ice Bear

THE ICE BEAR

THE
ICE
BEAR

by Betty Levin

Greenwillow Books, New York

Library of Congress Cataloging-in-Publication Data
Levin, Betty.
The ice bear.
Summary: A girl from the Land of the White Falcons, a bear
cub, and the bakerwoman's helper become pawns in the
power struggle which rages in the kingdom of Thyrne.
I. Title.   PZ7.L5759Ic 1986   [Fic]   86-254
ISBN 0-688-06431-0

For Jennifer and for Annie

Contents

THE ICE BEAR

PART I

THE LORD
OF MISRULE

1

"When the King's away," muttered Gunni as she pummeled the dough with angry fists, "the Lord will play."

Wat did his best to stand up to her. "Think of all the bread you will sell. You'll profit from this day."

"Profit?" She flopped the dough and pummeled some more. "It is the King's bear they will kill, not the Lord's. No one will profit but Havel, Lord of Urris." She swung her head over the floured board; her braids whipped from side to side.

Gunni was the only woman in Odstone to plait her hair in four braids like a lady of the manor. She bore them proudly, with a touch of defiance. Wat could never understand why she had to flaunt them. She was only the baker's widow. If she offended the Lord or his Steward or even the Bailiff, she might be denied this house and her livelihood. That put Wat's uncertain position at risk, too. Today he would work hard to sell her loaves and cakes in town. Maybe then she would remain here in the bake house, out of sight.

He would work hard for her, but he still pleaded for time to watch the spectacle, the bear's ordeal. "I saw them come," he told Gunni. "This morning, early, on the hill." This would remind her that he had been out at dawn to gather brush from the hill waste for her ovens.

He had watched the Lord's procession winding along the road to Odstone. It was always thrilling to see the horses in their gorgeous trappings, the curtained litters supported fore and aft by

matched palfreys and carrying, he knew, the elegant ladies. Bringing up the rear of this splendid train, behind the clerks and servants and Men of Law, stood the royal bear in a dung cart pulled
by four oxen.

"Even at such a distance," he went on excitedly, "I could tell
that the white she-bear is nothing like the brown bears we sometimes see." He meant performing bears that were led into town
from time to time, sad-looking creatures with sore feet and
gummy eyes, the scruffy fur worn to the skin by ropes and chains.
The royal bear, high-shouldered and massive, had made the dung
cart shake and wobble on the road.

"Then you are witness to this seizing. You have seen enough."

Wat tried another tack. Everyone said that this event promised
to be extraordinary. Other trials were held at the customary time.
But once the bear was caught, no one could think of keeping it
until the regular court convened. Havel and the Men of Law had
ordered a trial by combat. They had chosen Odstone for this trial
because it was a border town and more enclosed than any other in
Urris lands. The road from Odstone to the north became a haz-
ardous track through mountainous country that harbored bands of
outlaws. There was a new gate between the old stone pillars. It
closed one of the last gaps in the wall that surrounded the town.

But Gunni was not impressed with the extraordinary occasion
or Odstone's good fortune. Wat supposed he should have remembered how she had jeered whenever Clydog the Constable or the
Lord's Bailiff assured the townsfolk that the wall they labored on
was for their own protection. There was no pleasing her about it;
even now when it had brought the ice bear and all the people
streaming into Odstone for a look at it. People who would soon
grow hungry and pay good money for her bread.

"The Mirth Mongers have come," he told her. "There will be
mummery and dancing and tumbling when the bear and bear-keep
are finished. Everyone in all the Urris lands must be here," he
insisted, as Gunni set the dough to rise and drew a peel of

wheaten loaves from the best oven. Wat inhaled the delicious aroma and gazed in wonderment. The crusts had been stroked with egg yolk to give them a burnished look, like Gunni's golden hair. She seldom made such bread. Most folk could afford only the oatcakes or the round, flat barley loaves. This would be sold for a high price to noblemen and ladies, to the Lord himself.

"Everyone in Urris lands," Gunni agreed, "and more. If the Lord of Urris keeps seizing crown lands, half the Kingdom of Thyrne will be his. It will take a deal of baking, then, to feed the people of Urris."

Wat sighed. That wasn't what he was talking about. Couldn't Gunni think of anything else but the Lord's misrule? "There is a place for me on the hay wagon. I can see everything from there."

Gunni stopped to look at him. "Isn't it enough for you that we will gain a few extra pennies from these doings? Profit, as you say."

"But I may never see an ice bear again. They say it is the most dangerous of all beasts." Seeing a frown forming on her face, he added quickly, "Think of the story you tell me."

"I am thinking of it," Gunni told him. "It is one I heard from my mother. That monstrous bear had the mind and speech of a person. It trained the king's warriors and led them in battle. Then the warriors grew bearlike, savage and terrible, so that no man dared face them."

Wat's heart pounded. Every time she spoke of it, he thrilled to that bear. "Maybe," he wheedled, "this bear is the same as the one in the story."

"It is the same in one respect," she retorted. "It is a royal beast. Any who take part in its killing must answer to the King of Thyrne."

"But it is not without cause," Wat pressed. "Everyone speaks of the game it has killed. It is well known that the punishment for hunting in the Forest of Lythe is death."

"The bear and her cubs were sent to the forest on the King's orders. And don't tell me that the Lord of Urris acts on the King's behalf. That is nonsense. It is nothing short of robbery for Havel to bring the royal bear to justice, an ice bear worth a king's ransom. You may be sure that there will be a reckoning when the King returns. Take no part in this thing, save selling bread. That is the only right way for you to spend the day. Now," she finished, having dealt with his plea, "when the wheaten loaves are cool, take them straight to the marketplace. I'll send the girl to the alehouse with the oatcakes."

"The girl!" Wat was astonished. There she sat, just as she had done since coming into the bake house. "Does she know where to go? What money to ask?"

"She knows a deal more than you realize," snapped Gunni.

Wat eyed the girl's flat, foolish face. He doubted she would return, with or without bread money, but that was Gunni's concern.

Gunni took in his shrug of dismissal. Her voice dropped. "You shun her still. I thought you might be glad to share your space here with someone smaller than you."

Of course, Gunni was teasing him. Once he had let slip his longing to grow big. She had reminded him from the lofty height of herself that there were advantages to being small.

"Yes," he had spat out. "It is useful for climbing inside a potter's oven."

Gunni had paused a moment before responding. "And the leader of the Mirth Mongers, the one you admire? A small fellow, that Dodder, but there is none better."

Wat had nodded to that. It was true. But Gunni's teasing had nothing to do with Dodder of the Mirth Mongers and little to do with the idiot girl. As she never spoke, there was no way to guess whether she was small for her age like him or simply younger.

Wat stared openly at her. Her tongue did not protrude from her mouth, but otherwise she bore all the features of the town idiot, a lad called Snaill, who had drowned in the millrace. The girl's skin was darker than Snaill's, her black hair thicker than his sparse fringe. Yet she had the same kind of hands, broad and clumsy-looking, and those curiously curved eyes with drawn lids. Even more strikingly similar was her face; it held no expression at all. If she was going to stay, she could easily take Snaill's place as the idiot of Odstone.

Gunni said, "Make yourself useful while the bread cools. Fetch a bag of flour from the mill."

Wat groaned. That ended any hope of sneaking a moment for himself before selling bread. "What should I bring the miller?"

"Why, a flour sack. Tell him there will be a loaf by and by."

Gunni's dealings with Ulf of the Mill were mystifying. Most people brought either grain or money or both. As for Gunni, she made a notch on the wall for every sale to show the Bailiff, who collected the Lord's portion of her earnings. She drew circles on a board to mark her extra workdays and made slanted lines to keep track of her stores of grain. Yet she never accounted for the bread that went to the mill or the meal that came from there.

That must mean, Wat thought as he left the bake house, that Ulf probably kept no written account of his dealings with Gunni, either. As Wat trudged on, he could hear the shouts and cheers from the center of town. He supposed the onlookers had made wagers on the bear or the bear-keep. It didn't matter which won the bloody contest, for the survivor would be pronounced guilty and promptly hanged. What mattered was being there in the midst of the excitement and seeing the show of a lifetime.

Wat had not far to go. The bake house was near the river, away from most of the other houses, all of them built of sticks and mud and thatched with rushes. No one in Odstone grumbled over being forbidden to bake at home, for if one house caught fire, all the rest would burn. They brought their dough to Gunni or else bought bread from her. They were also forbidden to keep grinding stones. Clydog the Constable said this was to make certain that no one broke the bread law, but it was an added hardship on those who had to pay still more to have their oats and barley ground at the mill, the Lord's mill.

Wat did not have to go down to the south gate, for the wall was not complete at this end of Odstone. He could cross the small orchard and make his way around Nag Nook Corner, past the tannery, and then turn out of town to the river.

Usually he heard the mill before he came to it, but today the cogged wheels were still, the huge stone suspended. Wat was surprised to find Ulf sitting quietly and staring into the millpond. If he wasn't at work, why wasn't he at the center of the excitement in the marketplace?

Ulf hauled out a sack of flour and took Wat's empty one in exchange. Wat looked up at him. The odd pillar stone that gave the town its name was said to be more than two times taller than the tallest man in Odstone. Everyone agreed that Ulf was the man to measure by.

"She says there will be bread later."

Ulf nodded. Then, at the sounds of uproar coming from the crowds, he said quietly, "This day will be remembered."

Not by me, thought Wat. It will be like any other, as far as I am allowed to know it.

"Go," said Ulf. "Gunni will need all the help you can give her." He rubbed his bare arms, raising red hair and white dust.

"Must you stay here?" Wat couldn't imagine anyone willingly missing the bear fight.

Ulf smiled grimly. "I expect a visit from the Steward. There is money to collect, and no doubt he will advise me of some new stranglehold on the people of Odstone. Havel forges laws like a smith making bands of iron to hold barrel staves."

What was Ulf talking about? At this very moment there was a bear combat right inside their town.

Ulf ran his fingers through his thick red hair and plowed up flour into a cloud that settled on him all over again. "Odstone is the barrel," he said. "All of Urris is. The band tightens. Soon the staves will crack."

"Oh," said Wat, hardly hearing the man. More carping, just like Gunni. It had nothing to do with this important occasion.

In disgust Wat grabbed a corner of the bag and tried, like a man, to throw it over his shoulder. Of course, he couldn't. Of course, the miller saw his puny effort and offered to help load it on his back. His face aflame, Wat pretended not to have heard the offer. He stumbled off as fast as he could with the dense bag dragging and jouncing behind him.

2

Wat gripped the cloth that covered his basket so that no one could snatch a wheaten loaf. Thieves would be sifting through this crowd the way they did at fairs, filling their pouches with stolen goods. Usually they waited until a victim's eyes were fastened on a juggler or tumbler before sidling close, grabbing, then vanishing in the throng. Wat sometimes thought about joining a band of young thieves and learning their clever ways. But fair time came each year before the cold, dark days of winter. He was never quite ready to give up his place in the bake house or the hope that one day the Mirth Mongers might invite him into their troupe.

Everyone was talking at once. Trying to listen, Wat pushed his way through the jostling crowd. Was it possible that he had missed nothing?

It took him a while to sort out what had happened. It seemed that the man pitted against the bear had refused to fight. Even when the she-bear, crazed at being separated from her cubs, hurled herself to the length of her chain, he would not raise the cudgel. The cubs had risen up on their hind legs, big beasts the size of young bulls, just like curious spectators. And that was all. Neither bear nor bear-keep could be prodded into combat. By and by they would both be hanged.

Beside the odd stone, the Lord and his advisers were thick in conversation. The special booth reserved for members of his household had been erected on the mound that supported the pillar stone. Everyone there was astir, but Wat caught a glimpse of the ladies in their fine gowns. One of them was yawning.

A young maidservant came elbowing down to Wat. She asked for three loaves, which she wrapped in her apron. Then she darted back to the booth.

"You must pay," he called after her.

She disappeared behind the ladies.

"Thief!" he shouted.

All heads turned. The Lord himself and his Steward, the Men of Law, and Clydog the Constable, all looked down at the boy with the wheaten loaves.

Wat thought: Maybe I have angered them. He thought: Maybe they will feed me to the bear. He opened his mouth to protest, to explain, but no words came. Slowly, with deliberate unconcern, the Lord and his advisers shifted their attention away from Wat. In the next moment they had resumed their private discourse. Wat was forgotten.

He moved on. No matter how many baskets of bread he sold, he could not make up this loss. Gunni was hard on him when he came back short. Once a dog had jumped him and sent his oat-cakes flying. The dog had seized a cake and led him a chase. When he gave up and returned, all the fowl of Odstone seemed to have arrived ahead of him and were finishing off the rest of the cakes. Gunni had sent him to work at the salt house in addition to his work for her. She kept him at it until he had earned a fair amount of salt for her baking.

But this was different. He should have been paid. The Lord's Steward would still take half the cost of every loaf Gunni baked. It was thievery, pure and simple, and it made him feel angry and helpless. Quickly he sold the remaining loaves and returned to the bake house.

Gunni was angry, too, but her anger seemed like more of the mood she was already in. "It is past time for the King to come home," she declared. "Things like this happen because there is no proper ruler in the Kingdom of Thyrne. Soon all the poor folk will be ruined." She gave Wat more cool loaves to sell and handed the girl another basket of cakes.

This time Wat would avoid the Lord's household. He would offer his bread to tradespeople with horses. They had money enough for wheaten bread, and they always paid. When he returned to the bake house with his money bag clinking, the girl was back inside again. He watched her sprinkle flour on the board. For all the clumsy look of her, the flour sifted evenly, without waste. He hoped she would be good for harder work as time went on. She might wash the sacks in the winter when the water turned his fingers blue. She would not feel the aching cold. There was no such thing as pain for idiots because of the emptiness inside them. You could tell that just by looking at this girl. Her expression never changed, never showed the slightest feeling.

The cries and shouts from the center of town mounted. From the uproar Wat guessed that the hanging was about to begin. He started for the door, but Gunni was there before him.

"You are not ready with more loaves. I will come back soon," he promised. "After the hanging."

"No!" Gunni glanced over at the idiot child, who was licking flour from between her fingers.

"All right," he bargained, thinking Gunni minded his leaving the girl behind, "I'll take her. It will be a sight for her, the bear-keep and the bear."

Gunni swung a floury hand and clouted him hard across his head. "Not another word," she snapped.

Wat's ears were ringing, but he was more shocked than hurt. And baffled.

Bending down, Gunni grabbed him by the shoulder. "Her father," she whispered. "The bear-keep is her father."

Wat's head whipped around. The child had finished licking her fingers. She was squatting, her shoulders hunched; she looked like a little lump of dough. No need to whisper, he thought. There was no understanding in the girl's eyes or the set of her body. He turned his look to Gunni, a look full of questions.

"She came in the night," Gunni said softly. "Out of the Forest of Lythe. She had been traveling for days, only when it was dark. She was looking for her father and the bears."

He was aghast. "If they find her here, your house will be forfeit, everything . . ." It came to him that Gunni had sent the child to the alehouse on the town green. "They must already know she is here!"

"They know and know not. As the bear-keep never learned our language, he could tell them nothing. They thought the bear had eaten the child, and the Odstone folk think this girl a wandering idiot I took in and put to work."

Wat's eyes widened. How could Gunni take such a chance?

"Well and well." Gunni straightened. "Haven't I given you a place at my hearth since you came stumbling and crying off Runcorn Hill? You were all spindle-legged then, a spider blown from its web. And didn't folk think you were witless, too, until you found your tongue and gave voice to your few thoughts?"

Wat listened to her tirade and to the tumult of the crowds. He thought of the place saved for him on the hay wagon. All because of this idiot girl, he would lose the chance to see what remained of the spectacle. "The bear," he pleaded. "Just for that."

"Haven't I told you to take no part in this?"

"It is not a part I ask for," he cried. "I want the sight of it, nothing more."

In sudden fury, Gunni wheeled and flung the door wide. Then she stepped out of his way.

He hesitated. His ears were still ringing. Was she giving him his freedom or testing him now, preparing to strike him once more? He felt caught between her fixed outrage and the open door. But the clamor from the marketplace was irresistible. Ducking his head in case her hand flew at him again, he bolted out into the wonderful, tumultuous afternoon.

But there was a thick, solid wall of humanity all around the marketplace. He charged with his head down, ramming between people wherever he could and trying to dodge their blows. No one would stop him for fear of losing an advantageous position in the mob. Besides, there was no room for chasing.

Where was the hay wagon? How would he find it when he couldn't see over or through all the people?

At last he caught sight of a bit of space around a knot of men who looked like ruffians. No wonder people made room for them. No one wanted to stand beside thieves.

But Wat had nothing to lose. Stooped and crablike, he scuttled under ragged elbows and between a pair of scabby legs. Squirming through, he felt something tumble over his shoulder and drop in front of him. As he broke away, he tried to nudge the object aside. It nearly tripped him, though; only the human wall kept him from falling. A good thing. If he lost his balance here, he would be trampled. As he groped for whatever it was he'd stumbled over so that he could heave it aside, someone from behind booted him fiercely and slammed him against a cart wheel. Clutching the thing he had grabbed, he rolled under the cart and out of reach.

The dark beneath the cart reeked of something worse than pig offal. He rubbed his stubbed toe and bashed head and bruised backside. Then, cautiously, he crawled a little way out the far side and peered up. A cry stuck in his throat. He was underneath the she-bear and her cubs.

She was enormous, her fur not so much white as the color of corn stooks. And it was matted with blood and dung. He pulled himself out a little farther. Now he saw that she was clasping her cubs so tightly that nothing of their faces showed. Hers did, though. The sloping head narrowed to a black snout. The jaws parted enough to show her vicious, gleaming teeth. When she shifted her weight, the cart creaked, and the cubs pressed closer. Wat saw a long slash gaping from her neck to her shoulder as she leaned as far as the chains permitted and began to lick some of the filth from her cubs' coats. Wat's skin prickled at the sight. His stomach clenched.

He watched a moment longer before pressing on. When the object he had picked up snagged around a post, he nearly let it go. Then he saw that it was a leather pouch, smaller than a drinking bag and larger than a purse. Backing up, he yanked it to him. If anyone claimed it, he supposed he would hand it over. But if he dropped it here, someone else was bound to pick it up. So he tied it to his belt and loosened his tunic to cover it and then looked around and saw the hay wagon.

It was jammed with children. Wat's friend Brunn was at the rear, high up on hay provided for the Lord's horses. He reached over to give Wat a hand up. Brunn's sister, Jennet, squealed as Wat rolled over her legs. Something hard inside the pouch had whacked against her shins.

Wat gazed all about him. The crowd was a patchwork, with every colored cloth in the world joined. He could see the gallows perfectly, the crosspiece lashed to the odd stone. He could see all the way down to the south gateposts and across to the north gate. From here it was clear that the few pillar stones standing on the outskirts of Odstone really did nearly ring the town. They were said to be all that remained of a great circle of standing stones raised by giants in a time gone by. The odd stone had been part of the circle then. But as the town grew, it had moved beyond it. While some stones had become gateposts, and others, some mere stumps, had been built into the wall, the odd stone was left to command the highest and most central position at the head of the marketplace—the odd stone that gave the town its name and its gallows.

Wat asked Brunn what was happening and was told that the man had just been hanged.

"It wasn't much to see," Brunn assured Wat. "He scarcely moved."

Jennet said, "They will put his head on the south gatepost. I'll never dare walk under it. The head will look at me."

"It's no different than others," Brunn told her.

"It is, it is." Jennet shivered. "I never saw such a face. And his hair like the old brown horse's, with the black strands all down between its ears."

A girl near them overheard. "They say he spoke to the bear. Magic words. He is full of bear magic."

"He is full of nothing," Brunn retorted. "He's dead."

Another boy spoke up. "Full of eels. They fed him eels, and he gobbled them live and flipping. I saw. And it's true about speaking to the bear. The man spoke, and the she-bear waited till he was done. Then she picked up the eels in her feet, with claws as long as my arm."

Wat saw huge, furred paws holding two faceless cubs.

"Eels!" Brunn snorted. "The ice bear eats stags and the Lord's horses and oxen. And people." He spoke with authority, like his father, who was in charge of the hay lands and managed this wagon.

"Well, it was eels this morning," the boy returned. "Then the bear caught the keg, and the cubs played with it. They rolled on the eel keg as though nothing was about to happen to them."

The children talked on until the crowd was parted to make way for the cart. Everyone craned to see. When the cart stopped in front of the gallows, men with pikes and poles surrounded it. The she-bear rose to her full height. The crowd was suddenly silent. Some of the men fell back, but others cast a rope loop over her head. Turning slowly, the bear scanned the throng. She seemed to be looking for one particular face among the hundreds. Slowly the rope around her neck tightened. It was attached to the gallows.

The bear snarled. Suddenly she twisted down, reaching to the cubs. Then the snarl was choked out of her. Grabbing at the rope, she snapped and could not close her mouth again. The crowd shouted encouragement to the rope handlers, who had to pause to unhitch the cart's side panel. While some jabbed at her, four men worked to drop the side.

Wat caught a glimpse of the cubs as they clung to the she-bear's hind legs. In the next instant, without seeming to have noticed the men at the side, the bear swiped out, first at one man, then at another. There were screams and howls of pain. The bear struck again and again. The terrible raking claws were not easily stopped. Even while she was drawn up by the neck, she lunged and dealt out death. Some men were able to stagger out of reach; others dropped beside the gallows.

Jennet clutched Wat's sleeve. She turned him, pointing. While all other eyes were fastened on the injured men and the dying bear, the cubs scrambled down from the cart, one after the other. They went the only way there was room to go, away from the crowd, away from the marketplace.

Wat slipped off the hay wagon. He was thinking about catching them before their escape was noted. It would make him a hero; it might make him rich.

On the ground it wasn't so easy to keep track of them. Wat ran where he thought they had gone. He wished he knew what bears were likely to head for. He kept on running, hoping they had not taken a turn he had missed. Think of being the finder, he told himself. Surely there would be a reward. He might be given work in the manor.

Something white dashed across the road, then came toward him. It looked as though the cubs were heading back. Were they confused? They were both wailing. If they kept on, they would come straight to the gallows. Then they would be seized and killed. He would have nothing to gain. He would be doomed to spend the rest of his life with little more than yesterday's bread.

Flapping his arms, he dashed toward them. One cub stopped,

but the other bared its teeth and kept on coming. That brought Wat up short. The cub turned then, whimpering and growling at the same time. It scampered back to its twin, and the two started away again. Keeping his distance, Wat followed. He thought of places along the way where he might drive them into a fold or a shed. Most of the town cows were out on the fallow land eating down the weeds. The sheep were on the upland wastes. All he needed was one empty cow shed in just the right place.

He began to form a plan. It involved the idiot girl at the bake house. She could not be entirely without wits, or she would not be able to sell the cakes for Gunni. If she spoke the bear speech like her father, she might be able to coax the cubs into a hiding place until the time came for him to produce them.

The bear cubs were tiring, but they skittered on, their hind legs flying almost sideways as they scrambled away from him. Wat was gasping, the pouch thing kept striking his knees, and his plan refused to grow. It came to him that Gunni stood in the way of anything he wanted the idiot girl to do. But now that he had chased the cubs this far, he couldn't give them up. Ahead lay Nag Nook Corner. If only he could keep them from turning out of town!

At the fork in the road the bears paused. He could hear their labored breaths. Hissing and waving his arms, he leaned in the direction of the mill and willed the cubs to head for Rake's End. To his amazement they did. Instead of escaping past the tannery to the hill, where they would be in full view of all their hunters, or to the river, where he would surely lose them in the rushes, they ran straight toward Stirk Close.

They seemed to know where he wanted them to go. Even as he swung wide to turn them into the yard, they slowed of their own accord. One still whimpered through its harsh panting. They shuffled past squawking fowl. The cow shed lay straight ahead. If Wat had any breath left, he would have held it. He willed them into the shed, but something startled them. They veered, taking the next opening. It was the doorway to the cottage of Stirk Close.

Wat did not move. He waited for shouts or a scream. He heard nothing.

He had no time to think. He just ran up after the bear cubs and slammed both top and bottom doors. That was it. No house in Odstone had windows. There was only a small hole in the thatch over the hearth. With a stick propped against the lower door, the cubs were trapped inside.

3

By the time Wat reached the bake house, he knew he could never manage the idiot girl without Gunni's help. Of course, that would entitle Gunni to a share in the reward, but it couldn't be handled any other way. He burst inside to find fresh cakes and loaves already cooling on the boards. It hardly seemed possible that after all he had seen and done, Gunni had carried on in her steady, determined way.

Just then the horn sounded from the marketplace.

"The bears!" he blurted. "The cubs! They ran off. No one noticed then. Only now. The horn is for them. I have them in Stirk Close cottage."

Gunni threw some more brushwood on the fire. "What do you mean to do with them?" she asked.

"If they could be hidden. Couldn't the girl keep them quiet?"

From the sound of things outside, much of the throng was charging up Runcorn Hill. Soon people would be flocking this way as well. If Gunni took too long to think, the cubs were bound to be discovered. Wat let out an anxious sigh.

Gunni nodded, not to him but to herself. "The mill is the place," she said.

Wat was beside himself. "The cubs are not at the mill. They are in Stirk Close."

"Quick!" she ordered. "While I speak with Ulf, you take Kaila to the cubs. On the way show her how to bring the cubs to the mill." She gestured to the girl, who came to her at once. "Stay

with the bear cubs until Wat tells you it is safe. Then get them to
the mill as fast as ever you can. You must make them be still and
wait for you there. You must come directly back here so that I
may know as soon as it is done. Do you understand me?"

The girl nodded without speaking. Then Wat led her out to the
lane. They had to run, but that didn't matter, for everyone else
was running, too. The girl's short legs pumped so hard, Wat could
scarcely see them. He hated to take time to show her the path to
the mill. He hated to think of Ulf becoming another person with a
claim on the bears. With Ulf helping, Wat saw his own profit
dwindling even more. If only they could reach Stirk Close before
the cubs wrecked anything. At this moment the bears might be
eating all the Stirk Close cheese and drinking the ale put by for the
week, or making a shambles of the few utensils and clothes they
found. They could even be tearing apart the thatch to climb out
the roof.

He led the girl past the tannery and then down to the river
path. When they doubled back, he showed her how to stoop to
avoid being seen. He didn't want any of the searchers following
them to Stirk Close. He glanced over his shoulder to make sure
she followed his orders. There she was, trotting silently behind
him, her short body upright, yet nearly hidden in the tall rushes
that fringed the path.

Before approaching the cottage, Wat checked her and himself.
The girl stood in his shadow. They both listened. No sound issued
from the cottage. Running to the door, he opened the upper part
first. He could see nothing inside, nor hear anything, either. He
freed the lower door and beckoned to the girl. Then he opened it
just wide enough for her to squeeze through. Were the bears
there? He still heard nothing. And then, yes, a shuffling. A
whimper. The girl spoke, not ordinary words but a soft sound like
a croon.

He started to prop the stick against the door again, then
thought it might draw someone's notice that way.

"Can you keep them?" he called in a low voice. He waited a moment, but no answer came. He imagined her nodding her foolish head.

Remembering Gunni's directions, he walked away from Stirk Close toward the south gate. Maybe he would find the area clear; maybe he could send the girl off to the mill with the cubs before the crowds returned from the hill. He knew that if the cubs were caught in the open, everyone would try to be in on the kill. At that point he supposed he would take up a hoe or a rock as well. He might at least have a little bear blood on his tunic to show Brunn and the others.

The trouble was that if he looked toward the mill, he lost sight of the fork at Nag Nook Corner. He wandered one way, then, hearing voices, retraced his steps and tore uphill to get a better look below. He was peering this way and that when he heard a shout coming from somewhere near Stirk Close. Back he raced, arriving at the cottage as a small cluster of people surged toward the door. Wat joined them. They moved inside. He moved with them.

Clydog the Constable, pike in hand, approached the far corner. Wat pressed forward. There were the cubs. In the near darkness of the corner it was hard to tell where one began and the other left off. They were huddled head to tail. They did not stir. The idiot girl was nowhere to be seen.

Clydog jabbed at them. They turned their heads away from him and were otherwise motionless. It almost seemed to Wat as if they must think that if they could not see their attacker, they would be unseen as well. On came Clydog the Constable, arm back, pike raised. At the next jab one cub sprang, snarling at the pike. Everyone in the cottage sighed with satisfaction. At last they would have a show of combat.

The Constable swept his arm wide. He needed more room. Everyone stepped back for him. If the others joined in, Wat wanted to be ready, too. He felt along the wall behind him for something he could use as a club. Nothing. He freed the pouch from his belt. Maybe the hard thing at the bottom would give the pouch enough weight so that he could land a blow with it.

The Constable made a savage lunge. The cub squealed and fought back. The small crowd closed in again, waiting for a sign from Clydog. Their clubs and cudgels were in striking position; they were eager, watchful. Wat lowered the pouch. He could never get close enough to use it without putting himself within reach of those slashing claws. Anyway, all the biggest men had encircled Clydog and the bear cub. Wat was outside that circle.

Suddenly he thought of the other cub. He waited until all the men were taking turns around the circle before sidling over to the dark corner. He could hear the grunts of men and beast alike. From behind, the men looked like threshers beating kernels of wheat from the stalks. Soon there were no more snarls, only the pounding. If Wat did not get to the other cub in the corner, this one would be finished and the men would take over with the other.

But when he reached the second bear, it was so still, he feared it might already be dead or dying. It had been chased with its mother and twin; it had been hauled all over the place. Still, if he hit it now, no one need know that it could not move.

The cub's forelegs were folded at the chest, the paws tucked in. The sloping head was tipped up and into the darkness. Wat stepped closer. He would aim for the top of the head. He leaned over. There was the idiot girl, crouched between the bear and the wall, clinging to the white fur. Her eyes met Wat's, those queer-shaped eyes in the flat, expressionless face. The bear cowered against her.

All at once it came to Wat that he had more to gain than a first blow and a bit of blood to show for it. "Out!" he whispered to the girl. "Along the wall. Out."

For a moment the girl knelt there as if rooted. Then, her hand still gripping the cub, she crawled away behind the circle of men.

"Haste!" Wat said to her.

Someone in the circle shouted, "Enough. Save the skin."

"Haste!" Wat tried to call once again. But his mouth was so parched, he could only hiss. The girl and bear disappeared.

Long after the men dropped their arms and stood gazing down on what remained of the bear cub, Wat could hear their blunt-hard blows thudding in his head.

"Big as a bull," one remarked.

"Heavier," said another. "A fighter."

"They're all fight," declared a third.

Soon their boasting flagged. They mumbled about the danger they had all faced. They recalled the she-bear's attacks. Five men, at least, were dead. More were likely to succumb to the terrible wounds the she-bear had inflicted. Who would have thought that a bound bear could do such harm?

Wat wondered whether the girl had managed to get the cub to the mill by now. When would the men remember that there was a second cub? They were so full of this killing that not one of them thought of the twin. Surely the girl and the cub must be at the mill, unless they had been captured.

"Not an ordinary bear," Clydog the Constable was saying. "Not like any you ever saw before, nor likely will again."

The wife of Stirk Close stepped into their midst and bent down for a look. "I'll have some of the fur," she told them. "One of you with a knife cut me a few hairs to bury under the hearth."

Surely enough time had passed for the girl to reach the mill and return to the bake house. Quietly Wat edged toward the door. When they finally realized that the second cub was gone, there would be another chase. If he got away now, he need not join the hunt.

There was a crowd outside the bake house, too. What did it mean? Then he saw the dung cart and one thickly furred leg sticking up over the side. His stomach tumbled. He had to draw a deep breath before he could go near that cart. People who recognized him stepped aside to let him pass. He just glanced at the leg out of the corner of his eye and saw that it belonged to the she-bear, not the cub. He heaved a sigh and pressed forward.

Gunni was in the doorway, speaking with men from the Lord's household. She turned for an instant and called into the house. The idiot girl appeared. That must mean that the bear cub was at the mill, safely hidden. Gunni looked unconcerned as she bent down for a brief exchange with the girl.

But when Wat followed them into the house, he found that beneath Gunni's composure she was seething. She had to remove half-baked loaves from the oven in order to cook the bear's heart in their place.

A servant carried in a basin containing the bear's heart and liver and kidneys and lungs. He said they had not dared to put this organ meat on spits, lest it fall into the fire. There must be enough for all the noblemen. He told Gunni to make haste but to take great care with the heart. The Lord would share it with his favored companions, that they might all gain the bear's power from that eating. It would be well to cut it in many pieces, lest any at the table be deprived and take offense.

Gunni spoke shortly. She had heard all this before. Let Havel's servants and the bear carcass be gone so that she could get to her task.

The organ meat dripped and nearly quenched her fires. Soon the bake house was full of pungent smoke. Wat kept feeding the flames and wiping tears from his eyes. The stench was sickening to him and Gunni, but the girl did not seem to mind. She tested the liver with the tip of a cutting hook, then drew out the peel.

"It isn't done," said Gunni, preparing to slide the peel back in.

The girl held on tight. "Done," she said. "Enough."

Wat didn't know which surprised him more, hearing her speak real words or seeing Gunni give in to her.

For some strange reason the girl took no interest in the other organs, so Gunni left them in the ovens longer. Then, when all the meat was out on the boards, the girl took the hook, the same hook Wat used for cutting brush, and cleaved the heart. Again and again the hook cut through the meat, moving from the heart to the liver until one could hardly tell which strip of meat was from which organ.

Wat said, "She's getting them mixed."

Gunni, who was cubing the kidneys and lungs, did not seem to care.

As soon as the heart and liver, heaped and scrambled together, were returned to the basin, Gunni told Wat to take it to the servant who had ordered the heart for the Lord of Urris. "And do not touch the meat," she added. "Do not so much as lick a finger with its juices."

"What about her?" he asked, glancing at the girl. She was always licking flour from her hands. "Should she not be told also?"

"No need," snapped Gunni. "She will carry both baskets with the kidneys and lungs. After you hand over the heart, take one of the baskets and both of you sell the meat. Be quick about it."

"And return as soon as we are done?" He nearly asked her whether it was safe to pass the liver off as heart, but he supposed she judged the danger less than failing to provide enough heart for the Lord's feast.

"Return when she is ready," Gunni answered.

"Ready?" demanded Wat. "For what?" Why did Gunni treat the girl like someone to be reckoned with? After all, it was he who had followed the cubs and conceived the idea of hiding them and rescued the remaining cub. Now he was being ordered to wait upon an idiot girl.

"Do not let her out of your sight," was all that Gunni would tell him. Tilting a peel, she began to scrub away the meat juices with a handful of sand and ashes.

Wat led the girl up to the marketplace, where the Lord and his household and company sat at boards laid over makeshift trestles. In the gray nightshade of the early summer evening, the torches bound to the odd stone seemed to cast as much darkness as they did useful light. Pulsing shadows confused the eye with unreal motion. The bright surcoats and gowns worn by those at the table were reduced to somber tones. Even Havel's bright murrey cloth was dulled.

All around the marketplace folk were settling down for the night. No one traveled on the open road after sundown without strong company. A juggler came forward to perform before the feasting noblemen and ladies. His leathern balls seemed attached to invisible threads that tweaked each ball so nimbly that one after another of them leapt into the juggler's hand and as quickly out again.

It was hard to see the juggler's face in the shadows, but Wat thought he was one of Dodder's Mirth Mongers, a man named Teasel, who sometimes played with Wat and showed him tricks. Someday, he thought, he would take to the road again. Not as a potter's boy, not as a lead-boy to a blind peddler, but as a performer. He would juggle like Teasel and walk on his hands and vault into the air, suspended on invisible threads.

First he had to grow and prove himself. Holding the basin, a sudden thought struck him. He could easily snatch a tiny morsel of the bear's heart for himself. He wouldn't need much for so small a body. Wat slid one hand beneath the basin and, with the other, fished out a strip of the meat. It took only an instant to tuck it inside his belt. Of course, he had no way of knowing whether it was heart or liver, but that didn't trouble him. If heart, he could only gain from it; if liver, he would lose nothing.

In the next moment he handed over the basin to the Lord's servant and reached for one of the baskets. Pleased with himself, he took some time to stand there, quietly enjoying the juggling. When a man caught sight of the meat in Wat's basket and demanded some, and another person helped himself to a cube of kidney from the girl's basket, Wat sent her across the marketplace to sell what she could. He would make his way along this side and around behind the table. If he sold his meat to the servingfolk in the booth, maybe he would catch the maid who owed him the price of three wheaten loaves.

He thought he would be able to keep track of the idiot girl while he sold his meat, but everyone rushed him, clamoring for what they thought was part of the bear's heart. No one would listen when he tried to explain that he carried other organs. Mobbing him, they wrenched the basket out of his hands and grabbed fistfuls of the meat. Dogs darted in among them, gobbling any piece that fell. Before Wat could collect himself, every bit of meat was gone.

As soon as the people went off to fight among themselves over the scraps they clutched, Wat retrieved the basket. Now was the time to eat his bit of bear heart. He took it between his fingers and popped it into his mouth. The taste was like the awful stench in the bake house. He tried not to think about it. It was such a tiny piece of meat, it was gone with one bite. He gazed down over the heads of the seated diners. The Lord of Urris had taken a huge portion of bear heart on his knife. At least he thought it was bear heart. Those men sitting near him followed their lord's example.

Wat supposed the idiot girl must have been robbed of her meat as well. He looked out toward the bystanders but did not see her among them. Someone piped a tune; a tabor joined in. As folk made room for the dancers, Wat saw with dismay that the girl was in their midst. She advanced toward the Lord and his company, straight toward them.

Not unkindly, the dancers tried to draw her in as they saluted Havel, Lord of Urris. They were a colorful lot, with ribbons and bells at their knees and wrists. When the idiot girl would not join them, they formed a semicircle around her. She took no notice. One after another of them moved in to jostle her or pluck at her sleeve, but she just stood there with the basket at her side and would not be budged.

There was nothing Wat could do without drawing more attention to her and making matters worse. The men at the Lord's table were too intent on their feast and too distracted by the music and ale to pay much heed to the strange-looking child who faced them. To Wat, who kept a nervous eye on her, she seemed as unmovable as the odd stone—and as separate. As the Lord and his company washed down strips of heart and liver, they clapped their hands for more food and drink. Ale sloshed all over the boards. Nutmeats were brought to the diners; blackberries and jam patties to sweeten their tongues and redden their lips.

The dancers stamped and twirled. Bystanders began to sway. Soon it seemed as if all the crowd was in motion, all but the idiot girl who had planted herself before the trestle and boards, her eyes fixed on those who supped. In a while the Lord and his company swayed, too, heads bobbing to the beat of the tabor. When one and then another pushed away and some clutched at their stomachs or throats, it was natural to assume the ale had taken hold of them.

Wat ducked out of the way as a Man of Law was led past, groaning violently. More than too much ale, thought Wat. Now the Steward lurched from the table; he stumbled like one gone blind and uncaring. The Lord sat on, but his hands swept everything from the boards, even his knife and drinking cup. His hands kept sweeping long after there was nothing left to fling aside.

The dancers danced on, and the piper played his tune for them. The bystanders swung their arms and tapped their feet and clapped in time to the music. The Lord of Urris half rose from the bench, turned, then dropped to his knees, retching. Wat could see him crumple and fall writhing to the ground.

It wasn't until the ladies began to cry for help that the dancers took notice and faltered. Astonished and bewildered, they drew together. The idiot girl was just raising her eyes from the shambles. She seemed in absolute possession of herself. She was looking directly at Wat now. For some reason he felt an icy tug in the pit of his stomach. A shudder passed through him. The girl gave a little nod, a slight shrug, and made her way past the dancers and out of the marketplace.

"When she is ready," Gunni had said.

Wat dashed from the booth. He had to force his way through the confused crowd. Finally he saw the small figure waiting for him in the lane. As soon as he ran toward her, she started on again. She stayed ahead of him all the way to the bake house.

4

Gunni seemed to sense that something dire had befallen the Lord and his company.

"Will they die?" she wanted to know.

Wat was stunned. Die? How should he know? Had the meat been poisoned, then? It couldn't have been. He had seen it cooked and cut. What did Gunni mean asking if they would die?

The idiot girl shrugged her square shoulders. "Some may," she said. "Most will . . . wish it."

Wat gasped. Her words had only a slight strangeness, a shape around them like the curve of her eyes. "Did she put a spell on the heart of the she-bear?" he asked Gunni.

"We cannot waste time talking now," Gunni told him. "You must take her and the bear away while all the town attends the sick." Gunni turned to Kaila and told her to fetch the bear cub.

Kaila slipped out into the darkness.

"Take them away where?" Wat exclaimed. "The Lord and his men will hunt us down. They'll hang us." The thought of being put to death as an outlaw collided with Kaila's remark about those who would wish they could die. There was something deadly about that meat. He could still taste the bit he had stolen. His tongue seemed coated with it.

Gunni thrust a bowl of ale into his hands. "Drink," she commanded. She broke a loaf of bread and set it before him. "Eat while you can. Your pack will be light, for you must reach the Forest of Lythe before the men recover."

"No, no," he stammered, "I cannot go away. Do not send me."
He wanted to tell her that he would die on the way, alone and
forsaken.

"You can and you must. You will have a goodly lead, for the
Lord's men will have much on their minds this while. And on
their stomachs."

Their stomachs? The bread stuck in Wat's throat. He could not
swallow. "They'll notice I've gone," he protested.

"I will let it be known that you took to the road, that you both
deserted me. No one will realize it, anyway."

"They will," Wat insisted. "They'll recall that the sickness came
with the bear's heart that I brought."

"All who ate the meat you and Kaila carried in baskets will
know it was good. They will soon understand that it was the bear
herself who took revenge on her killers."

Wat stared at Gunni. She had known. Something about the
heart of the she-bear. If only she had told him.

"Poison?" he finally managed to ask. "Something you learned
from your mother?"

Gunni shook her head. "The only other thing my mother ever
mentioned, along with the story of the warrior bear, was that once
in a great while one of those ice bears came floating to Firland on
a field of ice. And sometimes, from the same direction, but only
when the Frozen Sea melted, strange men and women in skin
boats came, too. They wore the white fur of ice bears, people with
dark faces and hair as black as raven wings. My mother drew pic-
tures of such folk. Once she made me a corn baby and dressed it in
rabbit skin and gave it the face of the sea folk. Kaila's face. I
guessed what she was when I first saw her. And then she told me
all I needed to know. Just now she told me about the bear meat.
Not the heart, Wat, but the liver. No man can eat it without falling sick and maybe dying."

Kaila entered with the bear cub. Wat shrank out of its way.

"Get used to it," Gunni advised. "It will be your companion for
many a day."

All the way to the Forest of Lythe? "The Lord hunts in the forest," he argued.

"He will not hunt again for a long time."

"Then what am I to do?" he demanded. "Sell them?"

Gunni was outraged. "I was done with selling folk even before I was born. It was enough to know that my mother was brought here a slave." She kicked three loaves of bread across the floor toward the cub and handed one to the girl. "When you came to me," she went on, "you stayed of your own will. Now you leave at my bidding. Yet you are no less free."

The cub sat with a loaf clutched to its chest. It mouthed the bread, then suddenly gobbled it like a greedy pup. The girl handed it another. Wat could see its eyes fastened on her all the time it ate.

"Free?" he questioned. "With these two?"

Gunni nodded. "In time you will feel it. For now you do what must be done, because I say so. Until they are safely on their way."

Wat swallowed another objection. Probably Gunni was speaking for the girl's sake. As long as the girl could look to Wat for protection, she would go along with him and manage the cub. How clever Gunni was to think of that. She would send word to Wat when it was time to reveal the cub. She might even wait for the King to return from across the sea. The King's reward would be worth a deal more than the Lord's.

He tried to send Gunni a knowing glance, but she was loading a pack on Kaila's back. She brought another for him to carry. The cub yawned. This cub, thought Wat, would not end up a bloody heap like its twin. And if the King did not return before long, at the least there would be its unsullied skin to fetch a great price.

Only what if he sickened? When would he know whether he had eaten the liver? "Could we not wait awhile?" he pleaded.

Gunni grabbed Wat's arm, her fingers biting into his flesh. "You must go now, and swiftly. Keep from the road. Listen to Kaila. She knows about concealment. Leave no trace of yourselves."

No trace of a white bear cub the size of a young ox? What had he started? He felt hot and cold all at the same time. Maybe it was the first sign of sickness. What if he shrugged off the pack and left the bear to its bloody fate? After all, he was free. Gunni had said so. But her pincerlike fingers told him otherwise. He was being sent at her bidding, driven out of Odstone into certain danger and hunger and confusion. He had no fond memories of the wayfarer's life, always at the mercy of bigger, stronger folk. If only Gunni would relent.

He searched her face for some way out of this. He saw nothing but her fierce determination. Feeling bleak and lost already, he set off into the night.

But the cub would not follow. It stood in the lane, swinging its head and sniffing the darkness.

"Come!" he commanded Kaila and the cub.

Kaila said, "The bear waits for her mother. For the brother."

"Then it will be found. We will be found, too. Do you know what they will do to us?"

Kaila shot a glance at him. Her eyes, smoldering coals in the dark, closed face, made him shiver. Of course she knew. She had mixed the heart and liver together with deadly intent. He still might be one of her victims.

Gunni spoke from the doorway in low, urgent tones. "You must not tarry."

Wat said in a rush of fear, "It won't come. This is hopeless."

"It feels hopeless, yes. You will teach it hope." Gunni said to Kaila, "You go first. Wat will tell you where to turn. He will come behind and flog it if he must."

Wat made a wide sweep around the cub. "Hopeless," he repeated.

Kaila approached the cub. She placed her hands on either side of the furry face until the swinging head was stilled. Then she laid her own head against the cub's. After that she turned abruptly and trudged up the lane. The cub whimpered. Without slackening her pace, Kaila called back over her shoulder.

Gunni spoke sharply. "Now. Run at it."

Wat waved his arms and hissed, but he still kept his distance. The cub gave a snort and shuffled after Kaila. Wat reached for the pouch at his belt and swung that, but the cub took no notice. All she wanted was to keep Kaila in sight. Maybe she thought Kaila was taking her to her mother and brother. The image of the huge she-bear clasping this one and the twin in her mighty hug caught Wat mid-stride and nearly took his breath away. He didn't know why it stabbed him like that. He didn't know what he was doing here in the stumbling darkness chasing after a white bear cub and a girl with the gift of bear talk.

"Not there," he called to Kaila as the cub plunged toward Tanner's Brook. "This way, this way."

"She's drinking," Kaila said from quite near.

Wat spun around. He didn't like her stealth. He would have to watch her as well as the cub. Would he dare to sleep? "We must go on," he whispered. "We must be away from the road by daylight."

Kaila slipped through the tall sedges. A moment later the cub cut a swath through the marsh. Yes, he nodded, without calling out, that way. Soaked and muddy, he set off again behind the plodding cub.

When the sky began to lighten, Wat had to give up the cover of the marsh grass and head uphill. He felt uneasy about crossing the road. They would be visible until they reached the wasteland above the fields. "Turn," he called ahead softly.

Kaila turned sharply.

"No, no." Forgetting about the bear, he scrambled up toward her to show her the way. At once the cub veered off and cowered in the weeds.

"Don't frighten her," Kaila warned. "Stay back. You can show me the turn with your hand."

Kaila went to the bear, which had rolled onto her back. Kaila reached out. The bear swung her head around, opened her mouth, and took Kaila's wrist in her jaws.

Wat gasped. The beast could bite the hand right off.

With her free hand Kaila pushed at the muzzle and gently cuffed the head. The cub released the wrist and stretched out full-length with her eyes closed. Kaila spoke once, then turned to go. Grunting, the cub rolled over onto her feet, shook herself, and sauntered on behind Kaila.

Wat heaved a sigh. His legs were trembling. He hoped they would carry him as far as Cauldron Rock.

He barely managed to climb the ridge of turf that enclosed the field of rye. The cub tumbled and slid down into the grain and began to feed on it. She slashed at the long green stalks and grabbed mouthful after mouthful of the half-formed heads. Kaila was only able to lure the cub away from her green feast with a loaf that she pulled from Wat's pack.

At last they gained the far end of the field, clambered over another turf wall, and began the long, slow uphill push. The sun climbed with them. Down below, the field steamed. The rising vapors veiled the hill, but soon the sun would burn the moisture off. The day would be long and warm.

By the time they reached Cauldron Rock, they all sank gratefully in its shade. By now Wat knew he really was unwell. His head pounded; his belly felt swollen and tight. He fell into a restless sleep, waking from it again and again, each time drenched with sweat. Finally he was so thirsty, he had to crawl away from the giant rock to look for berries. But the only ones nearby were green and as hard as pebbles. He was afraid of his thirst, afraid of the taste in his mouth.

He peered down to the road where bedraggled walkers and one slow oxcart made their way out of Odstone. There was no sign of searchers or of any intense activity. He slumped down at the other end of the rock, for the shadow had moved, and the sun set fire to his face.

The cub's growl as she stretched and lurched to her feet roused Wat. He drew himself to his knees.

The cub began to cry, her jaws gaping, her muzzle tipped to the sky. The thin, harsh wail poured out of her in an unending stream of pain.

"Keep her quiet," he ordered Kaila, who was beside her in an instant.

Kaila tugged at the head and wrapped her arms around the neck, but the cub could not be silenced. Anyone on the road would hear her. Anyone, it seemed, would hear all the way back to the odd stone.

"Beat her!" he rasped, clapping his hands over his ears. It could be a human voice full of abject terror.

All at once, after years of forgetting, he knew that he had heard it before in a clay pit where the potter had sent him to dig, where he had witnessed the selling of a little girl. He had seen her clinging to a woman, while two men yanked at her arms and prodded her legs. The men spoke in low, hurried voices, and it was all done very quickly, very quietly. Until the money was pocketed and the selling man had to drag the woman from the spot. The child began to shriek then, her voice strung out in a thin, helpless wail. The buying man had given her a shake, packed her under his arm, and stumped off to the road, leaving Wat with his spade poised, certain that the clay pit could never be emptied of that harrowing cry. He had stumbled back to the potter, his basket half empty, unable to explain, unable to speak. The potter's beating had helped to drive the awful sound from his head.

This time it is only a bear, he tried to tell himself. But how could so huge a beast sound so piteous? He wanted to rage against her. He wanted to kill her.

While the bear's shrill wail flayed the hillside, all around them the world seemed to empty itself of life. Birds fell silent. Not even voles or rabbits stirred the grasses. At last the bear began to hear that silence. There were stretches between her cries, lengths of waiting for answering calls that would never come.

Into those stretches Kaila poured a tuneless song. It flowed into the desolate silence and around the bear cub, until it seemed to

Wat that Kaila's voice had the shape of the she-bear hugging the cubs in her fierce and tender embrace.

Slowly the cub sank down, crouched. She pointed her muzzle toward Kaila, stretched her neck, lay her head in Kaila's lap. The cub stayed like that for a while, her eyes on Kaila's face, on the shape of her voice, so soft now it was little more than a murmur. The birds broke into song again; the grasses moved with life. The cub, spelled by Kaila and by her grief, gave in at last. Gave up.

5

They started again before sundown. Wat told Kaila they must not lose sight of the road. He knew that the Forest of Lythe was southeast of Odstone. He had sometimes seen folk coming down from it to the road, but he did not know the exact way to the forest. The distant road was their only guide.

Later it occurred to him that Kaila ought to know the way, since she had come from the Forest of Lythe. But she shook her head at that. She had not come directly.

"I was looking for my father. For the bears. I ran and ran. I did not know where I was. Then I came to the road and had to turn one way or the other. That is how I came to Gunni."

He believed her. She could have been describing his own flight all those years back when Gunni had taken him in.

By daybreak the air had changed. Wat paused to look around and gain his bearings. Far below them the road looped around a hillock and parted from the river. Behind them the steep wasteland merged with the mountains. Wat could no longer see the gorge that split the terrain to the east of Odstone. An unwary traveler heading that way in a fog might stumble to his death if he tried to bypass the town. Already the crucial landmarks were blurred. The gorge and the sheer rock to the east of Odstone would soon appear to be little more than foothills. And below the road, to the west, the treacherous marshes stretched all the way to the river. Little wonder that folk were reluctant to stray from traveled paths.

Full of dread, Wat plodded on. In his misery he imagined himself transformed, his head as large as his pack, his wavering gait like that of an old, old man. Every breath was torn from his throat. He could not fill his lungs. Yet he knew that if they did not reach the forest, they would be seen and taken.

He could not imagine what it would be like once they were there. The few folk who skirted its edges to cross from the royal hunting lodge to the grazing land above the Odstone road counted themselves fortunate to have escaped the outlaws taking refuge in the forest. Wat dared not think about those outlaws. Fearful that if he gave in to his exhaustion he would drop in his tracks, he staggered after Kaila and the bear.

They were like shadows in a dream, one white and the other dark. Sometimes, when he fixed his gaze on the moving white shape, he found himself lurching from side to side in clumsy mimicry of that strange, high-shouldered gait. Once in a while the bear halted to sniff the air and let out a plaintive cry, but it was muted now, an echo of the piercing wail.

That night it began to rain. At first it felt wonderful, for it washed away the sweat and cooled Wat's feverish body. But it wasn't long before he was chilled. His eyes kept closing. Whenever he shifted his direction, Kaila had to come around to him and turn him back on course. He felt her hands grip his jaws and knew that she was trying to stop his teeth from chattering.

It rained through the day as well. When they stopped to rest, Wat could not lie down. He just stood with the rain coursing over him. Kaila pushed something into his mouth. Thinking it was sodden bread, he spit it out. Then he realized that it was a handful of blackberries. He licked their sweetness from his lips, only to feel his stomach twist in a sudden spasm of pain. Clutching himself, he found that he was walking once more.

Still later he was stopped again by Kaila, who shoved something else toward his face. He smelled blood and warm flesh. He recoiled. Was she trying to kill him? He saw her throw a large portion of whatever it was to the bear. She herself gnawed on the remaining piece. The sight of her tearing strings of raw meat from a bone made him gasp and heave. If he had had the strength, he would have run from her. Instead, he dropped to his knees and bent over until his head rested in the soaking turf.

Kaila helped him to his feet, but he kept slithering and losing his balance. The ground felt different. Also different was the order of their going. Kaila was beside him much of the time, or behind him, propping him up. He noticed that the bear was closer, too. Once, when he lurched to keep from falling, he bumped into her. She paid no attention, as if she could sense his weakness and knew he could not harm her.

"Look ahead," Kaila coaxed him.

He tried to straighten, but his neck was locked, his head tipped down. Even so, he could not watch his step. He slammed his foot against a rock and pitched forward. He sprawled there on his face, groaning through his clenched jaws. He had thought his feet numb with cold until now. The one that had struck the rock felt molten, raw, useless. It made him think of the meat Kaila had devoured.

He tried to tell her to keep away, to leave him there, but his tongue refused to work and his mouth could not open. Kaila tugged at him; she tried to haul him up. He found himself on his hands and knees and stayed that way for a moment. Like an animal, he thought. And then he rebelled. Kaila might behave like an animal, but he was not one. He would walk like a man.

He gave her his hand and let her help him to his feet. The pain had receded by now. He simply felt uneven, with one foot frozen and the other burning. He hobbled a few more steps. He tried to wipe the mud and rain from his face. Squinting, he saw something dark looming out of the mist and rain. He made a tremendous effort to focus on the dark mass before him. He saw one leafy branch; it looked almost black. He saw tree trunks.

Kaila led him toward the darkness. He heard new sounds, twigs snapping, a rustling. His body began to fold again. He was so cold that he had to make himself small, to curl up like a caterpillar in a bed of moss. Think of something hot, he told himself. Think of the potter's oven. His hands made the shape for patting the mud and clay onto the dome of sticks. Think of making the oven and the hot reek of earth inside once the first batch of pots was fired. Remember how those in-curving walls contained the warmth.

It was the earliest sensation he could recall. Only later, after he had grown too big to crawl inside the ovens, only then, when the potter traded him to a blind peddler, did he understand that he had not always been a potter's child. The potter would get another, one small enough to crawl inside an oven without cracking it, and deft enough to retrieve the fired pots. By then Wat had grown up with scabs on his knees from crawling on live embers. Each time he had emerged from the hot, acrid clay to gulp the open air, he felt he had cheated the grave. So it was a mistake to think of that now; it only made him desperate to break free.

He woke in darkness and bewilderment in a bed so warm and close that for an instant he believed he was inside the potter's oven again, inside and too big and trapped. He lurched, his nostrils full of a stench that was nearly suffocating. He pushed with all his might. He didn't care what he had to break to escape from this tight, terrifying prison. Freeing one arm, he made a fist. He punched the dense, soft wall. It throbbed and rumbled. He punched again. The rumbling deepened and became a growl. He opened his mouth and let out a yelp. He would be crushed.

Kaila pummeled the white head to make the bear cub shift her weight. Part of Wat's tunic was caught beneath a furred haunch. Kaila hammered away at the bear until she rolled sideways and lumbered to her fat paws. Wat just sat on the moss and stared at the creature he had bedded with. Had Kaila meant him to be squashed or smothered?

"You are warm now," she said. "You will be well."

He didn't have the strength to point out that he might have

been killed. He said, "Yes," for it was true that both chill and fever were gone. He knew that as long as he was so feeble, he would have to rely on Kaila. He would watch his tongue to avoid provoking her. He would also watch the bear. Her warning growl stayed with him.

Kaila nodded approvingly. "It is fitting. You saved her. She saved you."

He nodded. If that was how Kaila regarded it, he would leave it at that. Other matters pressed, like food and water. But his mind and body refused to go any farther. He looked around at the dark green world of trees and brush. His hand swept the forest floor of lumpy mosses and bracken fern. Everything was wet. Yet a kind of warmth surged up from the leaf mold. Leaning back on his elbows, he tried to absorb what it meant to be there at the edge of the Forest of Lythe. "It isn't raining anymore," he said.

Kaila looked at him. There was neither surprise nor mockery in her gaze. She considered what he had said, her eyes never leaving his face. She said, like him, "Yes." And still without smiling, still like him, she nodded.

PART II

THE FOREST
OF LYTHE

6

At first Kaila stayed near him. Then she was gone for a while. Wat was content to lie on his back looking up into the treetops. He listened to birds and watched squirrels chase each other.

Later, when he had more energy, he would weave a grass snare and try to catch something. He had done this with Brunn in the little wood that was part of the wasteland outside of Odstone. They weren't supposed to catch birds, but most of the boys tried their hands at netting them. All the pots in all the houses of the town contained bird-flavored soup from time to time. But here in the outskirts of the forest where there were more birds than Wat had ever seen before, there was no cooking pot, no soup.

Kaila brought him water in a curved length of oak bark. The water was brown and full of black specks, but Wat drank it all.

"When you are stronger," she said, "I will take you to the pool. Now," she went on, "I go to hunt. But I will leave the bear with you. She will keep you safe."

Wat shook his head. "I would rather face . . . other dangers," he told her.

Kaila shrugged. "She will make it harder for me. She was just learning to hunt when my father and the bears were taken from here."

He watched Kaila and the bear walk off together. Kaila went quietly, lightly. The bear scampered all around her and made a great racket in the leaves and bushes. Wat felt a twinge of regret. He hoped the bear would not prevent Kaila from bringing him something to eat.

He dozed awhile, then sat up against a tree trunk. Brushing leaves and twigs from his tunic, his hand came to the pouch. Now, at last, he could find out what it contained. He loosened the string, tipped the pouch upside down, and shook it. The first thing to tumble out was a knife sheathed in fine-tooled leather. He held his breath as he drew the blade free. It was perfect. Running his finger along the hard edge, he marveled that he and no other possessed it.

There was also a flint, but no tinder. He saw that he could use the dull edge of the knife blade with the flint stone to make a spark. Next he unwrapped a tiny linen bundle and found inside it a small stack of coins that looked much grander than any he was used to. It occurred to him that if their previous owner had taken care to wrap them so that no one might hear them clinking in the pouch, they must be exceedingly valuable. Wat bound them up again. Then he looked at the last object, which was puzzling. Two flat boards, no larger than a man's hand, were fastened with a bit of twine. When he untied the twine and separated the wooden slabs, he found a square of parchment with writing on it. He stared at the words he could not read and at a blob of red wax with a strange figure and more words imprinted on it.

As he sat with these things spread out before him, his puzzlement gave way to uneasiness. Who would carry such a knife and heavy coins and written words? Only someone highborn, someone of importance. Wat's hands went clammy. He might dig a hole and bury all but the knife, or all but the knife and the coins. He thought back to those rough-looking men in the marketplace. Now he was certain that they had stolen this pouch. Stolen! Anyone found in possession of it would lose, at the least, his right hand.

A breeze stirred the leaves and flipped the parchment away from him. He lunged for it, fitted it back between its covers of wood, and shoved it into the pouch. Then he slipped the bundle of coins and the flint inside, too. He would not bury anything, not yet. He looped the sheathed knife onto his belt. He had never worn one before. If the bear should return now without Kaila, he would not shrink from her like a frightened hare. He would stand up to her, ready and armed, like a man.

When he dropped off to sleep again, he kept starting, half awake, dream shreds clinging to him like dead leaves. Once he rose up shouting, "Thief!" He could feel again the heat of fury and helplessness at the loss of the three wheaten loaves. Yet for some reason he heard himself declaring, "I did not steal them. I did not mean to." Then he glanced all around to make certain no one had heard.

A few paces from him a doe and a fawn stood motionless, staring at him. He was sure that their eyes were fixed on the knife. Not because it was stolen, he told himself, but because they sensed its power. Slowly he reached for the hilt. He knew that unless they walked up to him and presented themselves for slaughter, he could not touch them. He only drew the knife to show them he was a man to be reckoned with.

In a flash they wheeled and slipped among the shadows.

Much later Kaila returned with the bear cub. She had two rabbits and a hare. Wat couldn't help gasping in admiration. There wasn't a drop of blood or a speck of filth on any of the animals. When he remarked on this, she said simply, "I must have the skins."

Without thinking how far he dared trust her, he showed her the knife. She extended her hand.

He said, "It is mine."

She nodded. She was not concerned with ownership. He let her take the knife. She made small, neat cuts, then laid the knife aside. She looked like an animal herself as she crouched over the little beasts, but all she did was put her mouth to the cut and blow until the skin puffed out. Then she sank back onto her knees, gave a twist and a yank, and slipped the carcass free. Next she gutted it, tossing the innards to the bear. Soon she had three inside-out skins and three perfect carcasses.

"A fire?" she asked him.

Wide-eyed, he could only nod. Then he remembered the flint. At least there was something for him to do now. He found it hard to get the sparks to catch in the wet forest floor. Kaila waited patiently, swatting away the cub as it came sniffing at the carcasses. It seemed to take forever, but at last they had a good, small fire. Wat wanted to throw the meat right in, but Kaila insisted that they wait for embers. She made greenwood spits. She made the most delicious feast Wat had ever tasted.

As soon as Kaila finished eating, she set to work on the skins. One at a time, she stuffed each one with leaves and grasses and then made a continuous circular cutting around and around. The bear ambled over and began to nose at her work.

"No," she said to it.

Wat leaned over to swat the cub away. The bear, one paw already on a skin, her claws lodged in it, swung her head around and rattled a growl at him. Wat froze. He didn't have his knife. He kept his eyes on the bear's curled lip. Kaila, scarcely looking at them, spoke words that were either bear talk or magic. At the same time she reached out and cuffed the cub's head. The bear cub dropped down, her ears flattened. Kaila's hand cuffed her again and then rested for a moment in the thick fur.

Kaila said to Wat, "You must not trouble her when it is hot, or when there is meat."

"Give me the knife," he demanded. "Next time I'll be ready for her."

Kaila spoke with mild scorn. "That would be foolish."

"You don't think I could kill her?" he retorted.

Her level gaze met his rage. She said evenly, with a shrug, "It could happen. But it would happen the other way as well. She would kill you." She went back to work on the skins.

Wat, still seething, hardly noticed what she was about until he saw her pull at one end of a skin and come away with a long rope with fur on it. "What will you make of that?" he couldn't help asking.

"A snare. Maybe we will have pig for our next food." She began

to scrape the fur and stretch the rope of skin. It took her all the
rest of that day and the next. Even when they walked out to a sun-
filled glade to pick blackberries, she carried the skin ropes and
worked them with her hands or the knife or with her teeth.

Wat noted her achievement with grudging respect. He found
himself thinking of her as Kaila now, or the girl, not the idiot girl.
It was unsettling. Anyone could tell just from looking at her that
she was no equal to the children of Odstone, who belonged under
roofs, or even to the children of bondsmen and wayfarers. No
matter how deft she was with a knife or how quick to bring down
game, she was not entirely human. Bear-girl, he thought. He
could shift his regard in that direction without losing his own
place. Bear-girl. That was what she was.

When they started off again, the order of their going was
changed. Kaila was still in the lead because she knew the way to
the pool. But Wat could walk beside her now or just behind her.
The bear, having grown used to him, crisscrossed their path,
sometimes dropping out of sight but always returning with a rush.
And then, just when Kaila told Wat they were nearing the pool,
the bear bounded ahead of them.

"She knows where she is," Kaila said. "The cubs played here
much."

"Is it where you stayed when you lived in the forest?"

Kaila shook her head. "There was a cave. Farther. A darkness in
the forest."

Wat looked around. There was a darkness here, too. "I have
never seen such trees," he told Kaila. "It feels strange."

She answered without expression, "Strange, yes. In the land of
my people there are no trees at all."

Wat couldn't imagine an absolutely treeless landscape. He
thought he might grow accustomed to these massive trunks and
the high, leafy roof of the forest. But an endless open plain? There
would be nothing to stop the wind, no shelter from the sun or
rain. What kind of people would choose to live in such a place?

Kaila said, "I cannot look up. It makes my stomach turn to see the trees over me, over everything. It was like that for my father as well. That is why we lived in the cave, even though it meant hunting deeper in the forest. Even though it was like the first place they kept us, like the room of stone beneath the great house. That was where my mother died and where we sickened. I heard the men who brought us to this forest say the King had ordered us to be moved, lest we all die in the stone room. Here we began to live again."

Just then they heard a splash. Kaila broke into a run. Wat did not trust his legs yet, so he followed more slowly. By the time he came to a clearing and saw the pool glinting and dancing in the dappled sunlight, Kaila was kneeling on the bank and reaching out to the cub. Wat drew closer. Kaila was holding a little fish. And now the bear cub pushed away; she rolled and kicked up a spray. The pool was churned black, but the water that shot up was dazzlingly clear. Fish shot up with it, and the cub flailed and played, catching them and flinging them back into the pool and out onto the bank where Kaila grabbed them.

Wat could see that the cub was fishing for the joy of it. Yet when Kaila spoke in the queer bear language, the fish were hurled in her direction. One landed near Wat. Laughing, he hurled himself on it. "More," he shouted. It was glorious sport. He slipped into the mud and went splashing out toward the bear.

For an instant she seemed uncertain of him. Then she rolled and swam all around him. Wat laughed again. The white head with the black nose plowing a tiny furrow in the pool came his way and then dodged around him. The invitation was clear. Wat plunged after her in mock pursuit. He was no match. Her powerful forelegs propelled her out into deeper water. Wat, breathless and suddenly overcome with weakness, had to give up and quit the pool. But he was still laughing as he climbed up the bank. Dripping and feeling clean and refreshed, he watched the bear surface, shake the water from her fur, and dive once more.

They cooked the fish on a bed of wet leaves in a recess among the rocks that edged one end of the pool. Kaila and the bear had already eaten several raw fish, but Wat was ravenous again. He had to prod and test the steaming fish until he lost one to the fire. He minded Kaila's silent reproach as much as the loss of the fish. He wanted to tell her that her patience only goaded him and made him careless. So it was her fault really. Come to that, it was her fault that he was here at all, waiting for a few tiny fish to eat, and no bread anywhere, none of Gunni's barley bread to fill the craving hollow inside himself.

In the days that followed, they caught and ate more fish and snared many small animals in the rabbit-skin twine that Kaila made. Finally, using both twine and a pit, they caught their first young pig.

By now Wat felt well and strong. While Kaila worked the skins, stretching them, pegging some and soaking others in a brew of oak bark and water, Wat began to make brief forays on his own. Each day he pressed farther.

Kaila warned him that the forest depths harbored dangerous men who would shun a glade like theirs beside the pool. As long as there was food enough, they should avoid the dark hiding places at the heart of the forest. A bear could go without food for many days at a time, but now the cub must eat and eat to make ready for the next lean time. Wat should be glad that they were safe for now, and with plenty of game at hand.

He couldn't admit to her that he was at a loss. It was she who brought their food and prepared it and busied herself with tasks of her making. There were times when Wat would have welcomed a bit of trouble.

Kaila showed him where the wood opened into a grassy clearing. The bear cub liked to graze there. So did deer. It was a relief to look out over open land again, to hunt for berries warmed by the sun. They surprised a majestic stag, which went bounding away downhill, only to double back again to seek the cover of brush and trees. Wat caught Kaila's measuring glance.

"No," he said, "not deer. Don't you know that it was the she-bear killing deer that made all the trouble for you in the first place?"

Kaila said, "We were brought from the stone room and let loose in the forest so the bears would not starve. People had been complaining because their goats and sheep had been taken to feed the bears. I heard the King's men speak of the trouble. We did not know that there would be other trouble when we hunted the deer and pigs."

"Killing royal game was the second trouble. The first trouble was and is between the King and the Lord of Urris."

"I do not understand about kings and lords, for there are no such men in the land of my people."

"Who rules you, then?" Wat asked in surprise. He could understand someone like Gunni without a king or lord, but Kaila was so different. She had no sense about laws and customs.

"The bear does," she answered, "when it comes to be killed and eaten. The walrus does, and the seal—"

"What is walrus?" Wat interrupted.

"A beast like . . . like a sea boar, only bigger than any pig. One of the beasts of our land. Like all the rest, they tell us where we must live and whether we will live or die."

"Well, that's not the same," he told her. "You do not have to obey."

Kaila shook her head, her shiny black hair lapping her shoulders. "We do. Obey and honor them. Especially bear."

Wat snorted. "Honor and then eat them?"

Kaila nodded. "When they wish to be eaten, they let it be known. Afterward the skin is hung with food beside it. It may not be touched until the bear spirit goes away, or else he will not come again and we will go hungry."

"You and your father did not eat the she-bear and her cubs when you were hungry. Is that because they did not want to be eaten?"

"They were like children." Kaila scowled. It was hard for her to explain. "Like brother and sister."

"That great she-bear?"

"When my father killed her mother and found her and took her into our house, she was much smaller than this one is now. When she grew to this size, she began to go away from time to time, but she always returned to us. And then, when she was fully grown, she brought the two cubs after a long winter away." Kaila paused. She seemed to be searching for more words. "Some of your people come to our land. They do not live like us. They come to buy our furs and walrus tusks. They wanted such a bear, one who walked beside us and waited with us beside the seal hole in the ice. I learned to speak your people's language. It helped my father deal with them. And when I told him how much they desired the bears for their king, my father, certain the she-bear would never allow strange men near her cubs, decided to bring them to the King of Thyrne himself. All of our people honored my father for his courage. There was a feast. We were very proud—" Kaila broke off.

"You came all this way," exclaimed Wat, "of your own will?"

"My father willed it. He thought the grateful King would hear his claim for our people. He meant to ask the King to call his men home. It is our land and our walrus and seal and bear, but your people frighten them off."

"And did the King hear your father?"

Kaila shook her head. "He was not there. Though it made no difference, because before we landed in this kingdom, we were all taken captive. So my father had no gift to give the King of Thyrne. He himself was given, along with my mother and me and the bears. Given to the King, who was not there to receive us."

Wat felt the sun prickling his arms. There were tiny red spots on his skin. He looked at Kaila's brown hands, her smooth, dark face. It seemed that even the sun could not reach her. Her expression was as smooth as her skin. And she spoke of those events as if they had happened to someone else or a long time ago.

"When did you come?" he asked.

"The summer before this one. The cubs' second summer. This she-cub is now three summers grown."

They both regarded the bear, now stretched on her back, lazily snatching grass heads and stuffing them into her mouth. As if aware of their gaze, she turned her eyes on Kaila and stopped chewing. Like a sister, thought Wat, mulling what Kaila had told him. Slowly it came to him that people and creatures might be bound this way, without ropes or chains or even laws. A new, strange thought to go beside the new, strange sounds of the forest that he was just beginning to recognize and place.

7

From time to time they returned to the high meadow to pick the raspberries that grew in prickly sprays among the tall grasses. The wary deer kept out of their way, but they could see where they had grazed. Wildfowl came, too, especially in the early morning. Kaila made a rawhide sling and brought down doves and blackbirds with stone shots. It looked so neat and quick, Wat couldn't help being envious. At least there was no one to see how skillful she was.

Only he wasn't certain of that. More and more often now he had a feeling of being watched. Kaila, too, sensed a presence. She would whip around suddenly to stare into dense undergrowth or hurl a rock into a clump of bushes and then stand perfectly still to hear what she had flushed. The twisted branches would spring back and then tremble and go still. There was nothing, nothing there.

The bear was no help at all. Either she was alarmed by a beetle climbing through the moss or else intrigued by a family of pigs rooting noisily at the base of an oak. There was no way of predicting her reactions, for they were as changeable as a fitful breeze.

The feeling of being watched was strongest under the great oak close to the pool. Maybe because of its vast, spreading branches. Maybe because of the old stories of men who changed themselves into oaks to muster their inhuman powers. The feeling baffled Wat. He did not like to think about magic powers. It was hard enough to understand the human power of men like the Lord of Urris or Clydog the Constable.

The bear had begun to hunt on her own. She stalked mice and voles. Occasionally she caught and ate them, always with a look of surprise. She was that way with the fish, too. She might paddle shoreward with a fish flapping in her mouth and then change her mind before Kaila could wrest it from her. Wheeling, she would utter a warning grunt, tuck the fish down under her, then gobble it up. Usually, though, she stood up in the shallows and flung the fish ashore. When she tossed one Wat's way, he went sprawling after it before it leapt back into the water. The bear remained upright, water dripping from her furry head and forelegs, watching him with an air of cautious interest. But she would not let him approach her unless she was swimming and could dodge around him.

Wat couldn't help thinking what a fool she would make if she were a performing bear. She was so clumsy at one moment, and so supple the next. She could make a stone laugh. He imagined himself swaggering into the marketplace of Odstone with the ice bear in tow. She would be wearing a muzzle of fine-tooled leather even though she was still a cub. Folk need not know she was not full-grown, for she was already larger than ordinary dancing bears. He would not have to jerk at the lead line, but only turn his hands so, and so, to set her twirling and tumbling.

The scene was so real to him, his shoulders tensed and his fingers twitched. He glanced over for another look, but she was hauling herself out onto the big rock across the pool from him. Maybe if he taught himself to swim with her, she would invite him to play again. Then he might begin to teach her real tricks.

Peering down, he tried to guess the depth of the water not far from the bank. He was afraid of sinking. He thought of Snaill in the millpond with the water closing over him. If Wat walked into the pool, how long could he keep his footing?

Something caught his eye beneath the surface. It was a wavering fan of whiteness. A fish? It couldn't be. No fish that size could live in the murky bottom. On his hands and knees, he leaned out over the water. The white thing was there, but it was motionless now. Perhaps it was just a rock, a flat white rock. His eyes were slits, shutting out sunlight, trying to focus on the thing. It looked like a giant fin. No, not a fin. A wing!

Wat drew back. Had he ever heard of underwater birds? He could only recall a tall tale about a flying fish. Feeling behind him for the long stick Kaila sometimes used across two forked ones to dry her skins, he dragged it forward slowly until he was able to poke it into the water. At once the smooth surface broke into ripples. He prodded harder. Mud came silting up from the bottom. Sighing, he sank back on his heels and waited for the water to clear.

He wished Kaila were with him. She might know how to dislodge the thing in the water. She could dig out ground squirrels and moles and badgers, all creatures that lurked in dark places; she could unearth covert nests and dens.

He squinted once more at the winglike thing in the pool, only to see it shatter as a small branch fell splashing over it. Startled, he could not be sure whether he saw the wing recoil or only imagined it. No, he was almost certain it had moved. So it was alive. "Ha!" He chortled in triumph. It was not often he came across something new before Kaila did.

"Ah . . . aah," came a strangled reply.

He peered into the water, but he couldn't see it anymore. "Where have you gone?" he exclaimed.

"Nowhere. Here. I fear I shall drown if I let go."

"If you haven't drowned already," Wat said, "you should be quite safe." What manner of thing could breathe and speak beneath the water?

"But I cannot get back. And—" There was a tearing sound. Another leafy branch crashed and then bobbed on the pool's surface. "Aah . . . aaaah!" The voice was very close.

Perplexed by the disembodied words, Wat said, "And what?"

"And," wailed the voice as more leaves came floating down, "I cannot swim." The next moment something whitish and large plopped down and landed with a huge splash in the water.

With good reason, thought Wat in amazement, for there, flailing in the shallows, was the largest and most bedraggled bird he had ever seen. It was too helpless to be frightening. Wat held out his stick and pulled the gawky creature to land. Its feathers hung limply; its skin sagged; its bare, rather hairy legs stabbed the water and broke through only to stab again as it sought solid ground. At last the bird came shaking and gasping toward Wat. Only it wasn't a bird exactly, for it had fingers. Wat could see them very plainly, still clutching the stick. Not clawed feet but human fingers. And the bird's face was almost human, too.

As it stood dripping before him, it patted the feathers of one wing, or arm, and then smoothed the other. Then it glanced nervously over its shoulder at the bear cub, which had been lolling in the sun before this. Now she clambered to her feet, her eyes on the creature that had staggered out of the pool.

The birdman retreated shakily in the direction of the oak. It seemed to embrace the rough trunk. Then it heaved itself, took a sort of hop, and collapsed at the base of the tree. "I cannot," it whimpered. "All this water in my feathers."

"Could you just fly up?" Wat suggested.

The birdman threw Wat a mournful look. "You mock me."

"Well then, must you be in a tree just now?"

Gazing at the bear cub gazing at him, the birdman said, "I feel safer in a tree."

"The bear will not bother you," Wat assured him. "Not," he added, "while I am here."

"Still, it is the better place to be. I am used to trees."

Wat was beginning to wonder what manner of creature the birdman really was. His spindly legs and wizened face showed every sign of decrepitude, but his voice was more like that of a young child than an old man. Or bird.

"What are you?" Wat asked him.

"Fallen," came the answer. "I am fallen from high places, as you must see. If you give me a boost, I think I might gain that limb."

Wat cupped his hands for the birdman to step into. Feathers brushed against his lowered head. While they were mostly white, Wat could see a few blues and greens and grays, as well as some with black bands and others speckled. Beneath this motley the birdman wore a patchwork garment with many rips and holes in it. Wat was afraid he might tear the flimsy thing, but the birdman was so light that Wat was able to thrust him upward at the first attempt. Almost at once the birdman had grasped the limb and was seated astride it. Shaking first one arm-wing, then the other, the birdman set to work straightening his feathers.

Gazing up at him, Wat declared, "You are not a bird."

The birdman peered down at him, his head cocked to one side.

"At least," Wat faltered, "at least you seemed . . ."

"It takes time," the birdman confided as he resumed his preening. "And practice. You cannot take flying lightly. Yet lightness has much to do with it. It is a great puzzlement." He rubbed his backside. "A sore trial."

"Were you trying to fly just then when you fell in the pool?"

The birdman straightened. "When I fly," he said with dignity, "it will be a noteworthy occasion. No, I was not flying. I was simply watching you as I have been doing these past days. There seemed to be something exceptional there in the water. You were drawn to it, I thought. I was curious. I forgot myself. I had climbed the hemlock to reach the high bough of the beech tree. I hoped to slip unnoticed from hemlock to beech, for their branches cross each other."

"I did not know that."

"Yes. You notice very little, you and the bear. The girl sees much. It is strange that she seldom looks up."

"That is because I am unused to trees," said Kaila, who had just appeared.

"Where is the great bear and the man?" he asked her. "Where is the other cub?"

"They were killed," Wat answered for her. To Kaila he said, "You never mentioned this . . . person."

Kaila regarded the birdman. "What is he?" she asked.

"Don't you know him? He knows you."

Kaila shook her head. "What kind of person is it?" she asked again.

Wat wished he could tell her. The creature was his discovery, so he must show some knowledge of it. "Fallen," he said. "Fallen from high places." It was the only reply that came to him.

They both stood beneath the oak limb studying the birdman as he arranged his feathered garments and spread himself to dry.

Overhead, the leaves rustled. A magpie squawked and flapped off across the pool. High up, Wat saw a white bird of prey drop to the topmost branches. The birdman glanced up, then raised his hands, cupping them together. Something plummeted through the branches, bounced from the limb, and thudded to the ground at Wat's feet.

Startled, Wat jumped back. The bear cub loped up to the thing, scooped it in her paw, and retreated growling.

"Stolen!" piped the birdman. "You let the bear make off with my meat."

"It was yours?" Wat blurted.

"Of course it was. You saw my falcon send it down to me."

So the white bird was a falcon. And one of great size, by the look of it. "Will it get you more?" asked Wat.

"Not likely. Gyr is not coaxed into favors. He performs them at his liking."

Kaila said, "I have rabbits. You will have some in a while."

She waited until she was close to Wat at the fire before telling him in an undertone, "There are such men in the land of my people."

"You have met a bird person like that?"

"Not to know," she answered. "But they are spoken of. They

will take one shape in the daytime, another at night. They have much power. They have Sight. They can bring game and they can banish it. We must take care. We must feed him well."

The cub had joined them, too. She sat on her haunches, away from the smoke, her eyes on the rabbits. Kaila scolded her in bear words for stealing the birdman's food. Undaunted, the cub kept watch over the sizzling meat.

Wat said, "I don't think the birdman expects us to go on feeding him. Only just this once."

Kaila said, "He can do us good. Or harm."

Wat knew better than to argue. In time Kaila might discover that underneath all those feathers there was nothing but a small, thin man. Unless, of course, the birdman was some kind of enchanter. Wat shook off that idea. What enchanter needed to be boosted into a tree? For all the wing feathers attached to his arms, the birdman was no less earthbound than Wat and Kaila.

When the rabbits were roasted, she carried them back to the oak. She extended one on her stick, but the birdman could not reach low enough. Wat dragged over a stump, took the stick from Kaila, and climbed until the rabbit was near the bough.

"So much!" exclaimed the birdman as he pulled the rabbit from the stick.

"Too much," muttered Wat.

Kaila cast him a sharp glance.

"Is it the bear's portion?" asked the birdman.

"The bear eats a deal more than one rabbit," Wat told him. "But she can fish, and we will hunt again." He avoided Kaila's eyes.

The birdman tossed a bone upward. The falcon plunged from its perch to pluck it on the fly.

"Must you feed the bird, too?" Wat asked.

"A token. Everything is shared."

Wat's heart sank. Did that mean they must also share? He had a feeling Kaila would think so. But the birdman was swiveling now and offering back more than half the uneaten rabbit.

"Is it not to your liking?" Kaila asked anxiously.

"It is excellent indeed. I have not tasted roast meat for the longest time. But a little is enough."

"You must eat when you can," she said. "Like the bear. To grow strong against the lean times."

"For me all times are lean," answered the birdman. "I cultivate leanness. When I have achieved the lightness of a bird, I shall fly."

Wat thought that would be a marvelous sight. He said, "I hope you do it while we are yet here."

"How long is your stay?" asked the birdman.

"I am not certain," said Wat. "Maybe until the King returns to Thyrne."

"Then you may well be here when I take to the air. Meanwhile we will grow to know each other very well."

"We will? Why is that?"

"Thieves and nobles alike speak freely as they ride through the forest thinking themselves unheard. I hear much. I do not think the King will soon come."

"But he must!" blurted Wat. "We wait his coming so that—" He broke off. Kaila's eyes were on him, deep and still. He was reminded of her look the night she watched the Lord and his company eating the heart and liver of the she-bear. "No, no," stammered Wat, "that is not what I mean to say. You see, Gunni, who sent us here, said . . . said . . ." But what was it she had said? Some command worded for the girl to hear, so that she would bring the bear and give Wat no trouble along the way. "Gunni is the baker's widow. . . ." Wat's voice trailed off.

"Said," Kaila continued for him, "we must seek cover in the forest. Said we must first hide. Later we will seek a way to escape this kingdom. I know we must cross the sea, but I do not know how to find it. Can you tell us which direction to take?"

The birdman pursed his lips. "What sea would that be?" he asked at length.

Kaila looked crestfallen. "Is there more than one? Then how can we find our way home?" She turned on her heel and trudged off to feed the remains of the birdman's rabbit to the cub.

"There appears to be a division between you and the girl," the birdman remarked.

"There is. She is ignorant. In most things ignorant."

"And were there two sets of commands, one for her and one for you?"

Wat had no intention of revealing the real reason for his being in the forest with a bear and a bear-girl. "Not two commands," he retorted. "What I started to say was an earlier plan, that is all. I forgot."

"Forgot that you were bidden to take that child and bear cub to their home across the sea?"

Wat flung his hands wide. "But it is hopeless," he blurted. "They are outlaws. She has no understanding. She believes she will go home."

"Believes in you, I warrant."

Wat kicked at a root. He did not look up. Never had he felt so trapped. He had to tell himself that this birdman had no power over him, no more than did Kaila and the bear. He had to force himself to recall Gunni's words: You are free.

8

As time went on, the birdman vanished and reappeared with such cunning that it did almost seem as if he could fly. Kaila, who believed that he did, was convinced that he changed his shape at will. That meant she had to offer him tasty morsels from every hunt.

On a day they had roasted a young pig and had eaten to their hearts' content, Kaila laid her succulent offering at the base of the oak tree. The glade was thick with the smoky aroma of the meat, so the birdman would know his portion awaited him. But since he must come in another form that they could not look upon, Kaila made Wat and the bear come away with her.

She guided them along a shaded path to a thicket where they could wait for the day to cool down before moving on to the steep meadow. But Wat stole off and doubled back to the pool. As soon as the birdman came for his meat, Wat would fetch Kaila and show her that the birdman did not change his shape.

There by the big rock that the bear liked to lie on, Wat drowsed and waited. He heard nothing but the hum of insect life all around him. Once he jolted awake when a frog plopped from the bank into the water. He could see the tiny wake it kicked into motion. A dragonfly hovered over the ripples, then whirred off into green shadows. Wat closed his eyes.

He sat up, then drew himself to his knees and stared across the pool. There was the falcon, standing on the meat, tearing off strips of it, pulling against its own grasp and weight. Wat sucked in his breath. He hadn't realized how big a bird it was. It was beautiful and terrible as it ripped the meat and devoured it.

He knew that if he shouted for Kaila, the falcon would take off. So he remained by the rock where he could watch it gulp down every bit of the birdman's portion. After that it spread its wings like a person stretching. The white feathers fanned out, revealing muted brown-gray flecks that faded and merged with the all-white neck and head. The falcon flapped noisily skyward, clumsy until it gained some height and swept free of the trees. Then it shot straight up where Wat, blinded by the sun, could see it no longer.

There was nothing to show Kaila, but he went to seek her out, anyway. If he could convince her that the birdman did not need her, she might be willing to move on toward the King's hunting lodge or northeast to the boundary of Urrisland.

"I saw what ate the meat," he told her as she lay against the bear's flank.

She sat bolt upright. "You should not. It is dangerous."

Wat laughed. "The falcon came and gobbled every bit of it."

Kaila nodded serenely. She sank back against the bear.

"Well then?" he demanded.

Pillowed in the creamy fur, she gazed up at him out of her bright, dark eyes.

"Don't you understand?" he shouted with exasperation. "No one came. Only Gyr the falcon."

Kaila bent her head in a languid nod. "Not Gyr," she said. "The birdman."

"The falcon. I saw."

"And the birdman? You saw him as well?"

"No, he was not there, or else the falcon would not have taken all the meat."

"You saw the birdman eat the meat."

Wat clenched his fists. Why was she so stubborn?

"In the land of my people," she went on, "we hear of a bear who takes a woman for his wife. At night he comes to her, a man then. But she must not follow him when he goes to hunt, for then he is a bear and very dangerous. When my people see a bear they think is that one, they drive their spears into the ice and let him pass. Even when they are very hungry. If they kill the one who is both bear and man, he will roar so loud that all the bears in the land and sea will hear and go far away. And so will the seal and the walrus. The people will have no food. They will die. That story is well known in my land."

"But this is not your land, and the birdman is not . . . is . . ." But what if there was truth in what she said? Could the falcon be the birdman's wife? Gunni's story of the warrior bear came back to him. He didn't know what to think. All he wanted to do was bring the bear closer to a place where the King might come when he returned to Thyrne.

Wat was just turning to walk away when the birdman came swinging overhead. Catching one limb after another, he propelled himself forward and downward. He seemed to be dropping to earth, but at the last instant he twisted around and pulled himself upright onto the lowest bough. "That was nothing," he declared breathlessly. "I knew you were watching. It never quite works when you're watching." He beamed down at them. "In spite of that, you know, it did feel like soaring. It really did, just for one moment."

"We left roast pig beside the oak for you," Wat told him.

"Ah," he said. "Pig makes a feast, especially cooked."

"If you like it so well," Kaila said to him, "I will bring you another."

"No, please do not bother. Not on my account. I eat so little. Like a bird, I trust. The more of me, the less I am." Seeing the beginning of a frown on Kaila's face, he added hastily, "Make no mistake. I am grateful."

Kaila nodded. "And you cleaned every last morsel? Wat said so."

Wat started to protest, but the birdman answered, "Yes, of

course. I am sure I must have, if he said so. As you know, my memory plays tricks with me. I am glad to know I wasted nothing of such a fine dish."

The bear had risen to her feet now. She yawned and then set off toward the meadowland. Reassured and smiling, Kaila followed her.

As soon as Wat thought they were out of earshot, he turned on the birdman. "Why did you agree that you had eaten the pig meat?"

"Was that a mistake? I thought she said . . . you said—"

"I saw the falcon eating the meat. She thinks—" He broke off. Maybe it would be unwise to mention what Kaila believed of the birdman.

"Well, if the meat is gone, I suppose that is all that matters. The child is so eager to please, I do not like to appear ungrateful." The birdman paused. Then he said, "I understand little of what she thinks, but I know what is in her heart. Her home. Going there. And I saw that with the man, the father, without understanding a word that he spoke."

"The language of her people," Wat commented. "Bear talk."

"I think," began the birdman falteringly, "that there are many ways of speaking. Yesterday I climbed higher than I have been before. To gain my bearings. To look for a sea."

Wat could not say that he had no real interest in the sea, unless the King's ship was on it bearing him homeward.

"I saw a road," the birdman went on. "Not the sea, but a road. It is remarkable how one thing leads to another, like a road going from town to town. I think I have lived in this forest a long while, all the time ignorant of myself, of my plight. Seeing the road made me quite agitated, and I felt sure I must fly somewhere. Instead, I had a nasty fall. See?" He extended his arm-wing to show Wat the ripped feathers, the broken pinions. "I went dizzy, and then I knew that I had fallen before like this."

"If you try to fly, are you not bound to fall?"

The birdman attempted to straighten the feathers. "True enough. Only I recalled a different kind of fall. I had the beginning of a memory."

Wat looked at him with interest. "Had you none at all before?"

The birdman wore his sorrowful air. "Only a sense of being banished, though for what deed and by what order I had not the slightest notion. I sometimes think that the falcon knows more than I."

"Do you speak bird language?" Wat asked him.

"I speak with the falcon, but it is in the language you and I use. Yet I have always known the falcon's name. Unless . . ." His face fell. "Unless I made it up and have forgotten that I did."

"Maybe remembering a little is like seeing a bit of the road. Maybe it will lead to more."

"I hope so. But that is what I came to tell you and nearly forgot to do. I recollected the way you must go. It is north. I am sure of it. North."

Wat heaved a sigh. "North leads to Odstone. We cannot go there."

"Odstone is just the first stop," the birdman declared. "That is what came to me when I gazed on that road. Beyond Odstone you will come to mountains and, after the mountains, the coast, the northernmost reach in the Kingdom of Thyrne. There are fishing villages there. And the sea, the first sea you must cross, but not the only one. Have you heard of the Islands of Tor? You will find your way to those islands, and then . . . and then I am not quite clear. There may yet be another land beyond, or there may be just the Frozen Sea. Is that not remarkable, that I can tell you so much of what you need to know?"

Wat could not answer him without revealing his own quite different intentions. He simply repeated what he had already said about the impossibility of passing through Odstone.

"You are too easily defeated," pressed the birdman. "You must strive, like me. I have set myself a seemingly impossible task—to fly. I seek no sorcery, no spell, only lightness and skill and courage. So must you gather your wits. If you wish to, you will think of something."

Wat nodded. All he wanted to do was to escape the company of this creature. He longed for ordinary conversation with an ordinary person like Brunn or Jennet. Even Gunni, who might tell him stories between the tasks she set him to. Between the bear and the bear-girl and the birdman, it was a struggle to think straight and to keep from despair.

Wat found himself toying with the idea of giving up the King's reward. It would be so easy to walk off and leave Kaila and the bear to fend for themselves. But if he did, nothing would be easy after that. A boy like him was bound to be caught or taken up by someone who would use him. The last time he had planned to run away, when the potter traded him to the blind peddler, common sense had held him in check. Even then he knew that he would not last long without a master. And when he did finally bolt, it was only because he had no choice.

That time there was no planning, no mulling. He and the peddler and other wayfarers had huddled for shelter in a burned-out hut. As usual, the peddler had started to babble. He always informed any who would listen about how the Lord of Urris had his eyes put out because he had seen the Lord's Steward taking loot from thieves. The punishment was supposed to be for stealing a rabbit from the Lord's warren, but the real reason was that the peddler could reveal the outlaws protected by the Lord. As the peddler jabbered on, Wat had seen a look pass between some of the travelers. One had asked why the peddler had no fear of spreading such a tale among strangers.

"What more can they do to me?" the peddler had replied.

In the morning, when the cramped, drenched wayfarers began to depart, the peddler lay quite still. What more could they do? They could strangle him in the night.

A woman with two small children had wailed in terror because they had sheltered with murderers. Then she had rummaged through the peddler's pack, taking what she could. Wat, not daring to interfere, waited until she left. When he was finally alone with the corpse and the half-empty sack, he had groped with trembling hands for the remaining goods.

"You will be caught robbing the dead," said a voice from overhead.

Looking up through broken beams, Wat had glimpsed a face blackened with charred timber. He supposed it was the face of a murderer, but he did not wait to find out. Like a hare running for its life, he had dashed out of the hut, darting first one way and then another, until he was able to hurl himself into a ditch and lie silent and unmoving.

When at last he had clambered over the upland waste outside Odstone, he could see the thatched roofs of the town, the gardens and orchards, the mill and tannery, the green and some of the old standing stones—all with a look that was solid and safe. He had pelted down Runcorn Hill toward a woman beating flour sacks beside the stream that fed the millpond. He had run straight to her, his heart drumming like a wild, hunted thing.

How many years ago? Nearly four. And never once had she threatened to sell him or give him up. She slapped him sometimes and often worked him so hard that at night he fell aching and exhausted onto his straw pallet. But the sleeping place was always there for him, always ready.

Until Kaila and the bears came and changed everything. Now he was free. Gunni had said so. He possessed a fine knife and money. Then what compelled him to continue to do Gunni's bidding? What reward was worth this loneliness, dwelling among mad folk, half human and half animal?

He felt as if his life had come to a standstill. Watching harvesters in the fields below the grassland, he recalled summers and autumns out in the town fields cutting and binding the tasseled barley with Brunn and Jennet. Their lives went on, their tasks dictated by the passing seasons. He supposed they were too busy to give much thought to him.

One day he found the fields of stubble full of sheep. His eyes swept the distant slopes until he caught sight of a shepherd and two dogs. Now the bear would have to be kept from the grassland lest the sheepdogs catch her scent. Maybe at last Kaila would see the need to move on into the forest.

But when he raised the matter with her, she insisted that they could not abandon the birdman. This time Wat argued with her. At least she must let the birdman say whether or not he cared about their staying. They went to look for him on the high ridge where he practiced his leaps into space. Beyond this gritty rampart that had the look of an ancient earth-wall, the land fell steeply. The dense forest bottom made a sweet cushion for the birdman's landings.

They found him poised with his winged arms outstretched. As he tilted forward, the arm-wings beat limply.

Wat couldn't keep from shouting, "Bend your knees. Move from the shoulders." He was recalling what the Mirth Mongers had taught him about tumbling.

The birdman turned a sad look on him. "I was trying to mimic Gyr. I have studied him long and hard. He spreads his wings until he stoops. When he comes straight down, he folds them partly back."

"You are not quite a falcon," Wat told him. The birdman looked so downcast that Wat quickly added something he had heard Dodder say to the other Mirth Mongers. "But you are right to think of the falcon. To pretend is to become."

"Would you show me what you mean?" asked the birdman.

"I have no feathers," Wat began to object, but he found himself flexing his arms as though they were wings.

"Neither have baby birds," said the birdman, "but they practice just the same. If you make the motions, then I will see where the arms and legs must go."

Wat bent and straightened. He shifted his weight to the balls of his feet and brought his shoulders back. He remembered the Mirth Monger's hand between his shoulder blades, at the small of his back, teaching him balance and the way to vault. And something else Dodder said to his troupe: To play a part you must be willing to be changed. They had played leap-the-frog on Odstone green. How Wat had sailed over one and then another, touching down only to spring once more. Like this. He pushed the ground beneath him; his body unfurled, reached, and rounded again as his feet struck the soft bottom and propelled him up a final time.

"Splendid!" cried the birdman. "You were truly airborne! Show me how to do that."

In a daze of joy Wat filled his lungs and let the tension drain from his legs and back. Then he set about teaching the birdman to bounce on his spindly legs. Again and again the birdman attempted to spring like Wat, but his arms were hopelessly constricted by the birdskin wings, and his head feathers kept flopping over his eyes. Yet when he finally collapsed, puffing and tottering in a tangle of legs and arms, his face glistened with heat and excitement. Nothing would discourage him. Eagerness and sadness possessed him alike.

The bear, who had been watching the lesson intently, wandered onto the ridge and peered over. Down she tumbled, bouncing and landing in a heap at the bottom. She came scampering back to the sound of their laughter. This time she flung herself from the ridge. Again they laughed and again she clambered back. Then she sat down and looked at them.

When the laughter subsided, Wat mentioned the sheepdogs. He asked the birdman whether he thought the bear would be safer deep in the forest.

"You prefer cutthroats and thieves to sheepdogs?" asked the birdman.

"We have been in the forest a long while without seeing any outlaws," Wat answered.

"Do you forget," asked the birdman lightly, "that all who live in the King's forest are outlaws? You are one. I am one."

"I mean," Wat explained, "the thieves and cutthroats you warn us of."

"Aah," said the birdman, as if the idea of such rogues was new to him. "Indeed, yes, you must avoid their like. They keep to the deepest parts of the forest and show themselves at its outmost limits only when they make raids on unsuspecting wanderers."

Wat sat up straight and drew his knees to his chest. He spoke distinctly, like one addressing the deaf. "I am thinking of the dogs. They are nearer than the rogues. They can scent the bear."

The birdman nodded. "I think you have little to fear from dogs who tend the sheep. It is the Lord's hounds that will find the bear, just as they did before when the bears and man were surrounded and taken from the forest." He nodded again. "Yes, you should be gone before the stag hunts begin. Only do not head into the forest, but out of it."

Wat gripped his knees and tried with all his might to keep his voice in check. "We cannot," he managed to declare in a choked whisper. "I have told you."

"You will think of something," the birdman offered cheerfully. He did not seem to realize that he had spoken those very words before.

"It is wrong to say that!" Wat cried out in protest. "It is misleading. Kaila will think—"

"Will think," the birdman concluded for him, nodding genially at the girl, "what she has thought from the start."

Wat dropped his head on his knees. It was a mistake to consult the birdman about this, about anything. Wat would have to puzzle out his next step by himself.

9

As the days shortened and cooled, the bear began to wander on her own. She seemed to be drawn toward the open meadowland. Wat feared that the sheep lured her. Kaila, intent on curing and sewing skins, just shrugged. It had happened last year when the summer waned; it had happened with the she-bear and her cubs.

"Maybe this cub is restless," suggested Wat. He almost added, "Like me."

"Restless?" Kaila threaded rabbit gut through the eye of her bone needle. She scowled and squinted all at the same time.

"Tired of . . ." Wat tried to explain. "Just tired."

"How can she be tired when she does so little?"

Exactly, thought Wat. But he could tell that the bear-girl would not understand. He tried another approach. "You must take her mind off the sheep. Take her into the forest, kill a pig."

"We have pig." Kaila nodded toward the strips of pig meat drying on the rack she had made.

"Another pig. It will amuse the bear."

Kaila removed the stakes that pinned a badger skin to the ground to stretch it out. "We do not hunt for amusement." She pulled the skin over a round stone. "If we take more than we need, the pig will not feed and clothe us." She beckoned to Wat, showing him that he must raise his arms to be measured. She was finishing a strange-looking jacket with an attached hood. Even before the sleeves were fitted to it, Wat had tried it on for her. He would be warm this winter, warmer than ever before.

Wat regretted that he had not learned more of Kaila's ways. Each time he had started to watch her, he had grown discouraged. Her stubby fingers were like extra eyes and teeth. Her silent concentration kept him at a distance, until finally he would walk away from her, convinced that he would never be able to turn a stiff, smelly pelt into a warm, supple garment.

This time Wat found himself heading for the leaping ridge where he had begun to practice some of the stunts he had learned from the tumblers in Dodder's troupe of Mirth Mongers. As he bent and stretched, the gritstone crunching underfoot, he thought he heard a moan floating up from below. Peering down, he saw nothing. He was beginning to think he had imagined the moan when he heard another that ended in a feeble gasp. He scrambled down the incline. Stooping, he swept the dense ground cover until his hand found a shoulder, a bent arm.

"Leg," gasped the birdman. "Leg first." He grunted as Wat hauled him up, his face ashen under leaf mold and needles. One leg was caught on a root and wrenched back. When Wat dragged it clear, the birdman yelped, grabbed the leg, and rocked himself in the nest of forest debris. With his mouth wide in a voiceless scream, he had the look of a scrawny baby bird.

If only he were as small as one. Wat tried to support him, but every time the injured leg touched something, the birdman collapsed all over again. It had begun to rain. The climb back would be slippery as well as steep. It was more than Wat could manage alone.

In the end he had to get Kaila, who came with the bear. While she and Wat struggled to boost the birdman uphill, the bear gazed down with her expectant look, as if waiting for them to include her in this new game. Growing desperate, Wat beckoned her. She came sliding on her rump.

"She will have to carry him," Wat told Kaila. "Make her lie here."

The birdman uttered a feeble protest, but Wat cut him off.

"You will not fly out of this ditch, nor walk out. So you must ride."

The bear sank down and promptly flopped onto her back. Kaila spoke sharply in the bear language. The cub groaned. The game was not turning out to her liking, but she righted herself and let them hoist the birdman onto her back. Her shoulders twitched. She flexed her paws. Kaila cuffed her across the snout and ordered her to rise. Both Wat and Kaila had to cling to the birdman as the bear struggled to gain a foothold.

By the time they were back at the grove beside the pool and the birdman had eased himself against the trunk of his favorite oak, they were all soaked and exhausted. The bear stretched out and eyed the creature she had carried. Like a cat, she extended one paw and slapped down a feather that had parted from the birdman's garment. She drew it to her mouth, only to spit it out at once. But some of it stuck to her tongue. Wat bent toward her to peel away the feather fragment. He could feel the heat of her as he picked a bit of quill from between her hard, smooth teeth. Her eyes were on his face. As soon as he withdrew his hand, she swung her head Kaila's way. Kaila spoke a bear word, and the cub bounded up. Hurling herself into the pool, she splashed and splashed.

"Washing away the feeling of you," Kaila told Wat.

"The rain should do that," he answered, holding his hand out to the downpour. Suddenly he closed his fingers. The cub's heat was still on them, her breath and teeth and tongue. Sheltering his hand against his tunic, he held what remained of her in his fist.

For days the birdman sat on the ground while the falcon and Kaila and Wat brought him everything he might need. Kaila made a soft cushion for his blue, swollen leg. She and Wat sat or squatted there facing him, making a circle within the circle of trees. And they talked.

The birdman's fall had jarred loose more pieces from his past. He described a ship on towering seas, though he could not yet recall where it took him. That made Kaila speak about the life she had lived with her father and mother and bears before they had sailed away from their homeland. Even though she used many words they did not know, Wat began to see the vast, windswept world she came from.

Her story of treachery came in fits and starts. Those who first advised and later betrayed her father had been so clever that her father had been slow to realize he was no longer free. When he finally understood, his heart was broken. To be a slave was worse by far than the unfamiliar food and the airless stone room and the sickness they all endured. Even after they were released in the Forest of Lythe, he lived his last days in shame.

"But he was bear-keep to the King," the birdman pointed out. "That is no small honor."

"He was not free," said Kaila. "He set out a free man with gifts for a king."

The birdman spoke with sudden intensity. "The King could not have known that. Those who deceived your father deceived the King as well."

The birdman's insistence puzzled Wat. "How can you know that?" he asked.

The birdman looked a little surprised. He pressed his fingers to his head. "How indeed? And yet I seem to. I am certain I know what manner of man the King is."

While Kaila and the birdman talked on, Wat picked up a stick. Idly he scratched a circle in the hard-packed earth. Seeing it as a wheel, he drew spokes. Only they came out wrong; they stood up from the rim of the wheel. Where they should have been he made a likeness of a hand. Then he knew that he had drawn a picture of the seal on the bit of parchment in his pouch. He couldn't help noticing how the birdman leaned as far as his leg would allow, craning, staring at the picture.

Wat got up and strolled off. The bear came padding after him, then veered, heading for the high meadow. Wat put out a warning hand as Kaila might have done. The bear fell behind him again, stopping each time he did, waiting for a command. It was thrilling to have her respond that way. Scanning the hillside and finding no sheep in sight, he let her out to browse on the upland grass. With the gleaning finished in the fields below, it would be safe again until plowing time.

The bear tensed. Very quietly she rose on her hind legs, her eyes on something downhill that he couldn't see. Glancing around for a way to get himself higher, too, Wat caught sight of a chestnut tree with good strong boughs not far from the ground. He jumped up to catch hold of one, but it was just out of reach. He clapped his hands to bring the bear beneath the bough. She came haltingly, but she allowed him to take hold of her shoulder fur. As soon as he dug in, she swiveled, and he had to begin again. This time she remained still. Using her shoulder to boost himself, he sprang up, flailed, and grabbed the bough. Gloating over his cleverness and his authority with the bear, he climbed as far as he dared.

He was high enough to see the road now. He shuddered with excitement and something like dread, for there, far below the forest and yet not so far away, a pack train crawled along the road. It looked like a procession of beetles and caterpillars, but he knew it consisted of carts and packhorses and people, all of them heading toward Odstone.

He wanted the bear to ease him down, but she was nowhere in sight now. He called to her, waited, and called once more. He wasn't stranded. He was able to jump down from the lowest bough quite easily, but he was annoyed that she had abandoned him without a thought.

He found her browsing serenely on cow parsley. She ignored his command to come away. He wanted to teach her a lesson as Kaila sometimes did, but when he raised his hand against her, she wheeled out of reach, her head whipping around to show her curled lip, her teeth stained green from the cow parsley. Wat dropped his hand. Glowering at her, he commanded her once more, and strode back toward the grove and the pool. He was nearly there before the bear came lumbering after him. He pretended not to notice her then. Flinging himself down in front of Kaila and the birdman, he told them about the pack train. Surely now it was time to move on into the forest.

"It must be close to fair time," remarked the birdman.

Odstone Fair! Of course! That was it! And then it occurred to Wat that the town gates would be shut while the fair was in progress, so that no one could leave Odstone without paying a toll. "It might be the one time we could get past the town unnoticed," he said. "There must be a way around the gorge above the town or through the marshland below it." He was so eager to move on that he was willing to give up the idea of going deeper into the forest. Even the road north seemed inviting after all this time.

But the birdman shook his head.

"Why not? You said I must think of a way."

"There is no way around the town. The Lord of Urris has seen to that. But do they not proclaim the Peace when the fair commences?"

Wat nodded. If the birdman found fault with his idea, so be it. He didn't want to go north, anyway. He only wanted to go somewhere away.

"And when they proclaim the Peace," the birdman went on, "are not all felons and outlaws allowed to move at will within town limits?"

Wat's jaw dropped. The birdman was right. No one could be held or punished while the fair was in progress, except offenders seized for crimes committed at the fair and brought before the Fair Court. If Wat could get inside the gates with Kaila and the bear, they would have three days without threat of capture. Three days. And afterward? "Not enough time," he said.

The birdman smiled. "You do not yet know what time you need. First you must decide what you will do with it."

Disgruntled, Wat felt like backing away from the whole notion. "It is what they will do with us I'm thinking of."

Still the birdman smiled. "You can train the bear?" he asked Kaila.

"What is train?" she asked. "People on the road with packs?"

"Like oxen under the yoke," Wat explained.

Kaila scowled.

"But to play," Wat added, excitement mounting, for now he saw where the birdman was leading them. "To play at your bidding."

"The cub will not refuse you," the birdman put in. "You will shape her like a mother bear."

Kaila shook her head. "There is but one mother."

"You must take her place, child. It is said that when a bear is born, it is a mere lump of flesh. The mother licks it into shape, gives it head and feet and eyes and nose. You will lick this bear into a performer."

"Is that something you just remembered?" asked Wat. "About the mother bear."

The birdman considered. "It is another thing I seem to know," he said finally. "And more, now that I think that way. The ice bear is like . . . like Gyr. The Land of the White Falcons!" He clapped his hand to his mouth. "What have I said?" he mumbled. "What am I saying?"

Baffled, Wat and Kaila waited for him to go on.

The birdman's hands dropped to his lap. "The King's bear," he whispered. "The King's hawk." In a voice still hushed but full of wonder, he said, "I am the King's Falconer. What am I doing here?"

Wat's heart leapt with hope. Here was a way to give the bear to the King. But surely the royal Falconer would be a man of substance. The birdman must be raving.

And the birdman did indeed seem to be muttering nonsense. "They must think I stole Gyr. Made off with the royal falcon. He came after me, and he led them to me. He is sure as an arrow, a white arrow that cannot miss its mark. They ran me to earth like a fox or badger. It is why I took to the trees—" He broke off, and then continued again, muttering to himself.

"Why would they harm the King's Falconer?" Wat asked.

The birdman turned his gaze on Wat. He pondered the question. He shook his head. "I only know," he finally said, "that I was fleeing for my life."

"From the King?"

"I think not. You see, there are many in the kingdom who claim to serve the crown, but they are in league with Havel, Lord of Urris. They will challenge the King when he returns to Thyrne. They already occupy lands they have no right to. They seize the King's rents. I have heard them boasting of their gains. When they came for the bears and the bear-keep, I heard them speak of luring a royal messenger from the road with the promise of showing him a better way. He carried a Writ of Safe Conduct for all of Thyrne, and when they were finished with him, they took even that. He was stripped and left to die." The birdman faltered, his eyes wide with remembered horror.

"What is it?" pressed Wat.

Tears streamed down the birdman's bony face. "Aah," he sighed. "Aaah."

Kaila brought him cool, fresh water from the pool. Kneeling, she dipped her fingers into her pigskin water bag and wiped away the tears. But more kept falling, and he would not speak again. Would not or could not.

In the days that followed, Wat and Kaila grew more and more anxious over the birdman's despondency. They turned to one another for ideas.

"Herbs," said Wat. "A posset to clear his mind and lift his heart."

"Show me," said Kaila.

"You are supposed to know such things," he cried. "It is woman's art."

Kaila picked meadow rue and rosemary. She stirred honey and

tiny unripe apples together, but she could not boil the mixture, for she had no cook pot. She set the wooden bowl in the sun. Bees and wasps came quarreling around it. Finally she stirred the concoction and dipped her fingers into it and then into the birdman's mouth. He swallowed the bittersweet liquor. He even smiled. But he spoke not a word.

The falcon dropped little doves and tiny mice beside him. Kaila took them away for their feathers or skins and returned them to him clean and supple. He smiled. He nodded. That was all.

"Think what made him speak so gladly," Kaila suggested to Wat.

"You mean about the fair?"

Kaila nodded. "Let him know you are following his advice."

Wat sat himself down beside the drowsing cub and prodded her into sleepy attention. He performed a somersault. "Like this," he told her, bowing his head. The bear tucked hers to her chest, then rolled over onto her side. "Like this!" he shouted at her. The bear rose to her feet and eyed him intently. This time he took the somersault at a run, flipped, left the ground, and landed on his feet. The bear backed up, wriggled her hindquarters, lumbered forward. She seemed to trip over her own paws. She landed with a grunt on her back.

Wat and Kaila sat on the ground and laughed. When they finally stopped, they heard their laughter echoing faintly from under the oak tree. Together they rose and sauntered over to the birdman.

He was still giving out little gasps and sputters with one word inside them. "Fool," he was saying. "Fool." Then he spoke to Wat and Kaila. "She is a mummer, that bear. She will make folk laugh. You have a Mirth Bear for the fair. Your money box will be full."

"I have money already," Wat told him. "The antics could be a way to bring the bear inside the town before the gates are closed."

The birdman said, "You will need more money than you know."

Wat backed down. But he thought of a way to keep the bird-man's interest and liveliness up. He fetched his pouch and emptied it beside the birdman. Now, at last, he might learn what the coins were worth.

The birdman was clearly shocked by what he saw. He turned the coins over. He set them down with care. "Worth," he said, "a nobleman's blood price. A man might buy his freedom and his chattel and his wife and children with this." He fixed Wat with a look. "How do you come by such treasure?"

Uncomfortable under that gaze, Wat told him. The birdman frowned.

"It was all by chance," Wat insisted, "not by thievery."

"Show me what lies between those wooden covers."

Anxious to mollify and please the birdman, Wat quickly untied the cord that bound the parchment. The birdman took it in his hand and stared at it for a long time. "The royal seal," he mur-mured. "The King's hand."

"You know what is written there? What the words say?"

The birdman cast him such a fierce glance that Wat fell silent. Finally, feeling accused, he muttered, "It wasn't meant to be thiev-ery."

The birdman sighed. "It was, lad. It was the property of one of the King's messengers, a Writ of Safe Conduct."

Wat was aghast.

The birdman nodded to himself. "He is sending his messengers round the kingdom to discover which lords are loyal and which plotting against him." The birdman clasped his head in his hands. "Oh, he must think me turned from him. He must think that of me."

"You will show him you have not been unfaithful. You will sit on the bear as you would your horse and come away with us."

The birdman smiled bleakly. "With the King's ice bear and his white falcon? How far would I get without their drawing notice?"

Wat refrained from saying that the birdman himself might catch as many eyes along the way. "As you must defend your honor," Wat declared somewhat pointedly, "you will think of something."

The birdman heard the echo of his own counsel. "Since you put it like that," he promised with a half smile, "I will give it some thought."

"And we should leave quite soon," Wat pressed. He was thinking that with the pack trains arriving in Odstone, all the able-bodied of the town would be cutting greenwood for the stalls and booths. He recalled those days leading up to the fair, days full of many voices and pounding feet. Soon Gunni would begin baking oatcakes and wheaten loaves and barley and rye bread.

"Let me think," said the birdman. He sounded weary, on the verge of silence again. "Leave me," he told Wat. "See to . . ." He waved in dismissal. "See to whatever it is you must do," he finished, as if Wat had already gone from him or was someone he hardly knew.

10

Alone with the bear, Wat played so hard that she became used to being mauled and vaulted over and climbed upon. She never tired of the tumbling. She would scramble to her feet, ready for more. Sometimes she became so excited that she hurled herself at Wat, but even when she knocked the wind out of him, her claws did not rake him. Kaila told him to cuff her if she began to mouth him, but the cub never went that far.

He grew bolder with her. Clambering onto her back, he rode her, at first splayed out, then sitting, and finally, tentatively, standing. It took all his energy and concentration to stay on. The bear, entering into the spirit of play, lumbered off without a care. Wat was smacked by branches and once, when the cub was hot and panting, dumped into the pool.

"When there are other folk about," Wat told Kaila, "you will have to stay close to the bear and keep her from mowing them down or plowing through booths and stalls."

Kaila did not understand what he meant, because she had never been to a fair and had never seen performing beasts. But she made the cub stand quietly while she fitted a rawhide harness to her for carrying bags of skins and dried meat strips and her specially prepared concoction of dried, pulverized meat pounded together with the pulp of berries.

She made a new feathered tunic for the birdman, with shiny raven wings stitched to the sleeves and shoulders. More raven feathers were attached at the back, with gray next and white after that, all overlapping and merging to a mottled white and gray across the chest. The birdman said it was far too beautiful for one who had not yet achieved flight, but he let her take away the old feather tunic to mend. Then he concerned himself with the pressing matter confronting all of them—a way to get the bear inside the town before the gates were closed, and out again when the fair ended.

Wat thought Ulf would be willing to hide them in the mill. They might slip into town in the early hours before dawn. But where could they stay after that? They must remain concealed until the Peace was proclaimed. The birdman stressed the need to join packmen and merchants loyal to the King, or Mirth Mongers jealous of their liberty. There might be some safety traveling in their midst.

Wat redoubled his efforts to teach the bear to perform at his command. He chose feats she already knew and attached words to them the way Kaila fastened feathers to the birdman's tunic. "Fish!" he would cry each time the cub tossed a fish his way, until suddenly she seemed to comprehend and began to throw her catch to him at his bidding. When she played the fool atop the ridge and went burrowing down the steep incline headfirst, he shouted, "Charge!" And after a while she would lower her head at his command and drive through the loose ground cover like a battering ram.

Finally, in triumph, they performed for the birdman, who clapped with delight.

"And she will easily carry you forth from here," Wat declared. "You need not fear her now."

The birdman shook his head. "I have thought much about it. I will not go."

"But why? It is all arranged."

The birdman said, "In a while hunters will come from Urris Manor. The forest will teem with men in debt to the Lord. It is here on the King's hunting grounds that Havel rewards his followers and makes new ones. While they chase the stag and boar, they will plot as they always do. This time when I hear them, I will have enough of my wits about me to mark each name and face. When the King returns, I will show him his enemies."

"But how can you get to him if his men think you are against him, too?"

"I will find a way."

If only Wat could make the birdman see that no one would lend an ear to such an outlandish figure. But all he could bring himself to say was, "You cannot approach the King's men. It is too dangerous."

The birdman wore his sad smile. "When I thought myself an outlaw, it seemed I must deserve my banishment. I believed I was guilty of so dread a deed that I fled my own self and so gave up my reason, my humanity."

"Do you recall the deed now?" Wat asked him.

The birdman shook his head. "Perhaps I ran from those who challenged me. Or maybe I crawled naked from a ditch, more fortunate than that messenger whose pouch you carry."

"You were set upon?"

"It is not all clear yet, but I suspect it was something like that. I hope when my memory comes whole that I will not find that I turned my back on a companion." He looked down. "Do you think I might have done such a thing?"

"No!" declared Wat. "Never."

"And what does Kaila think?" the birdman asked the girl.

She met his eyes. "The falcon sees the smallest creature in the air and on the ground. He sees everything. He followed you, serves you."

"Yes, because he saw how helpless I was."

"Because he saw a good man, a friend."

"But his nearness endangers you," Wat had to add. "Especially if you conceal yourself to overhear the Lord's plottings."

The birdman nodded. "But I am tired of hiding for myself. Now I will hide for a purpose."

After that, the birdman was like one who has drawn his will and settled all his debts. He was lighthearted in some ways, grave in others. He drew maps for Wat. Here were the islands of Tor, some of them visible from the north coast of Thyrne. There, beyond, lay Firland, named for its fiery mountains. The birdman had never been farther than that, but he knew of the Frozen Sea and the Land of the White Falcons, immense and trackless and cold. A cruel land to some, he warned. But to others, he added, nodding at Kaila, home.

"Unless you send the bear across the fields of ice, I think you must wait for a spring crossing. You will need a place to bide over the winter. That is why you should fill your money box at the fair. And the Writ of Safe Conduct will see you far. Do not let it out of your hands."

Wat nodded. He was still deeply uneasy about leaving the birdman behind. He had already resolved to leave the parchment with him.

When the time came for parting, they helped the birdman into the oak tree and made him comfortable with evergreen branches and rabbit skins. He seemed pale with the black raven feathers about him. His legs and arms had a brittle look that worried Wat, but the birdman put on a show of good cheer.

"I am sure I shall fly," he informed them, "just as soon as my leg is fully mended. Meanwhile, no bird was ever so provided for."

Wat stalled. The falcon was nowhere in sight. If something had happened to him, how would the birdman manage? "I must check the food bag," he mumbled, lowering it from the branch. Turning away, he bent over the sack, quickly withdrew the wood-covered writ, and slipped it in with the food. He would inspect the water bag, too, just to seem natural.

But the birdman ordered Kaila to fetch back the food bag.

"We should be on our way," Wat grumbled, as if the birdman were delaying them.

It was no use. The birdman suspected Wat and found the wood-clasped parchment, which he tossed down to the ground.

"Keep it," Wat implored. "You will need it."

"You have greater need. And farther to go. Unless," he added, fixing Wat with a penetrating eye, "unless you change your plans."

Wat had a feeling the birdman could read his mind as easily as he read the words on the parchment. "You know the plan," Wat retorted, "but no one knows what lies beyond Odstone and the next few days."

"And as no one knows what may arise and where your road must lead, let you take the Writ of Safe Conduct and be gone."

Wat packed it in his pouch. He could feel it against his thigh, a boon he would gladly be rid of. It seemed heavy with reproach and reminder, stolen but needed, a goad and a warning. Compared with it, the carrysack he hoisted on his back seemed to weigh nothing at all.

PART III
A FEAST
OF FOOLS

11

Once again they traveled by dark, but in a shorter time. They were strong and full of energy and could make use of the longer nights. But when they reached the outskirts of Odstone, it was harder to stay out of the way than before. Townsfolk roamed the wasteland, cutting wood for the fair. As it was the only time they were allowed to take greenwood, someone from every household gathered enough to hide away for winter use or to trade to the woodwright.

So Wat and Kaila remained behind Cauldron Rock and waited. A swineherd came near them on his way back from Middle Wood with all the town's pigs snuffling and grunting contentedly after feeding on acorns and roots. Then, just as Wat ventured out into the open, a knot of chattering children appeared with nets of grass and sedge. They were after songbirds to sell at the fair. Wat held his breath until they moved on.

Finally he made his way downhill to look for the safest route to the mill. But with so many folk streaming into Odstone, there did not seem to be a way across the road. To his dismay he found that the town wall had been completed. Now there was no hope of dodging around unfastened palings or hovering in the shadows of unconnected pillar stones. Everything was fastened, all connected. How then could they bring the bear inside the wall before the gate was closed?

A light rain fell. It left the ground spongy, the air sodden. Dawn wore a dismal mantle until the Mirth Mongers came around the bend at the base of Runcorn Hill. One of them lumbered and wallowed like a drunken beast dressed in straw. All at once Wat knew how to enter the town with the bear. They would have to wait out the day before he could put his scheme to work. And it must not fail, for tomorrow was the first day of the fair.

That night, while the town slept, he and Kaila made their way down Runcorn Hill, pulling oat straw as they went and binding it onto the bear's harness and pack. But it was one thing to put it on, another to keep it in place. The cub stood for just so much fussing, then groaned and sank down. Kaila scolded. The bear rolled onto her back and gazed up mournfully. She found a bit of straw with the oat head still on it, plucked and ate the kernels.

By the time the night sky began to pale, they had nothing to show for all their effort but patches of torn straw, useless for thatching now, and an edgy bear cub. The only thing to do was ask the Mirth Mongers for help.

It was still so dark that few were about as Wat made his way through the gate. But there was a drowsy porter with his back against the gatepost. Wat was glad he had not risked bringing the bear. Inside the wall, he paused a moment, fighting the impulse to turn downhill to the bake house. But he had to get to Dodder before sunup, so he headed uphill toward Tailor's Close, which was where the Mirth Mongers stayed when they came to Odstone.

Dodder was lying on his back with his head propped against the wall of the cow shed behind the tailor's house. Wat saw Spurge and Toadflax sleeping nearby. The others must be inside the shed, for the cows were all out on the mown haylands to graze down the weeds before the winter plowing.

When Wat touched Dodder, he sprang awake, instantly indignant and cross. Wat tried to explain his predicament. Dodder kept stopping him with questions that put Wat off his plea. Tense and chilled in the early-morning dampness, he was sure he was getting everything jumbled and wrong. He needed to convince Dodder how useful the bear could be to the Mirth Mongers if they would only bring her here.

Dodder finally hushed him. He was thinking hard, a calculating look in his eyes. Then he stood up and roused Spurge and Toadflax. After speaking with them, he ducked inside the cow shed. Spurge and Toadflax yawned and stretched. Dodder emerged with two others, Furze and Teasel. They would leave the women, Bedstraw and Nettle, and the child, Little Robin, to make ready for the bear.

Wat was shivering now. Someone thrust a surcoat at him. He put it on over his tunic, but he could not stop shivering. Dodder carried a roll of murrey cloth and a skein of scarlet ribbon. He told Wat to lead the way, and they all set off at a run. Wat called ahead as they neared the place where he had left Kaila. She materialized in the half-light like a rock come to life. The bear stood close to her, ready to bolt.

Wat threw out a hand. He warned the Mirth Mongers to move slowly now, quietly. With a flick of his wrist he summoned the bear. She darted anxious looks at the men behind him. "Come!" he commanded softly. She padded over to him.

"The bear trusts you," said Dodder. "So must we. Cover her with the cloth. It will draw the eye from the color of her fur and the shape of her. I myself will walk beside you. I worked with a brown bear once, a bear for dancing. I recall how long it took to forge the trust and how dangerous it was without. So," he went on, turning to the other Mirth Mongers, "two of you will go ahead and two behind."

Kaila and Wat drew the cloth over the bear until she was draped in purple. Kaila tied rabbit skins to her head. Dodder and the others nodded approvingly. "Like donkey's ears," said Teasel, "a fool's disguise." Then Wat wound the scarlet ribbon around the cloth, making it secure. The scarlet strips crisscrossing the purple made so bold a look, no one would have thought the troupe intended any sort of concealment by it.

Yet they were strangely silent as they approached the gate, a solemn procession with a brilliantly clothed beast in their midst, like a royal personage attended by courtiers and knights. Spurge began a song, which they all took up, their voices low but firm and measured. No one quickened a step. The song kept them all in check, their faces forward, their eyes keen and bright. There was not one guilty glance over a shoulder. Wat scarcely breathed. His head was full of the singing, although afterward he could remember nothing of the song itself, neither its tune nor the words that went with it.

When they reached the cow shed in Tailor's Close, the bear stopped and sat down with a definite thud. Wat could not budge her. He wished he could tell her that this place was different from Stirk Close where her twin was clubbed to death.

Kaila spoke bear words. They made another kind of song. Kaila sang the bear into the dark, safe hiding place and then curled up against her to shut out everyone and everything else.

It had been a long night. Wat knew they would sleep now. He was relieved when Dodder said the troupe would see the tricks and feats Wat had promised to show them later in the day. That meant he had time to go to the bake house now.

"Bring us bread," Bedstraw called after him.

"I will," Wat shouted back, confident now, gleeful. He pelted down the familiar lane.

Gunni must have been baking all night, for the boards were laden with little seed cakes, flat oatcakes, round barley loaves, and long wheaten loaves. How good everything smelled. How close and warm and sweet. Gunni was pulling a peel from the domed oven when she turned at the rush of air Wat brought inside with him. She stooped to lay the peel on the earthen, rush-covered floor. Then she wiped her hands on her apron, walked over to Wat, and placed her hands on his shoulders. The grip was hard, hot.

Wat said quickly, "The bear is safe. So is Kaila. They are sleeping."

There wasn't time enough to tell her everything or to hear all her news. But he noticed a grim, set look to her features and guessed that things must have gone hard for her over the summer and during the harvest. In all the time he had resented her bidding him away, he had never once thought how she would manage without his work. She told him now that Ulf of the Mill had helped with her share of work in the fields. She made Wat laugh as she described Ulf, a great hulk of a man, slowing to keep pace with the four reapers in his group.

Wat's head was heavy with weariness and the sudden, enveloping warmth. When Gunni laid a sack on the floor in his old place, he could hardly keep his eyes open long enough to make his way to it. He heard her remarking on the surcoat as she shook out the sack and smoothed it again. He was dressed too fine to be covered with flour, she seemed to be saying. He struggled to tell her he must soon be away to practice with the Mirth Mongers, but the words clogged and came out a mumble. He could hear her kneading and pounding another batch of dough. The sound was as familiar as his own breathing.

When Wat awoke, Gunni gave him a kettle of pottage as well as bread to take to the cow shed behind the tailor's house. There he found the Mirth Mongers trying to persuade Kaila that the bear must be muzzled for the fair. She had already killed and eaten one of the tailor's cockerels and had made a swipe at his dog when it came too close. There was no telling who or what might be next.

Wat was able to distract everyone with the bread and pottage. Then he took Kaila aside.

"Folk will object if the bear eats their geese or tears their mantles. They will fear for their children. They will be thinking of what the she-bear did to those men." He wanted to say that all those folk who had craned for a good look at the bear being hanged could easily be stirred like that again, but he knew that if he frightened Kaila too much, she might hold the bear back from performing. "It must still be fresh in their minds" was all he dared to warn her.

Kaila hung her head. She didn't give up, but she didn't argue anymore, either.

"It is only for a few days. You can make her accept the muzzle. She will do anything for you."

But once Kaila reluctantly agreed and Nettle fashioned a muzzle from hemp rope, the bear fought it. She pulled it down with her claws so that one rope slanted across her eyes. This made her frantic.

"Speak to her," Wat pleaded with Kaila. "Use your bear talk."

Straightening the muzzle, Kaila uttered bear words and crooned and rubbed the bear's neck. Dodder picked up a tabor and began to shake and tap it. Bedstraw and Teasel started to dance. Leaning against Kaila, the bear watched them. Spurge played on the pipe. Nettle and Furze joined the dance. Dodder beckoned Wat, who walked toward the dancers. It felt strange moving to the rhythm of the pipe and tabor. He clapped his hands, calling the bear cub with his wrists. Dragging the rope from her muzzle, she ambled toward him.

It was just the way it had been in the grove by the pool. The bear tried to mimic every exploit. Wat grew bolder and wilder because of the dancing around him and the music and the eyes, all those eyes watching. He sprang across the bear cub, then somersaulted onto her and off again with a spring that set him on his feet. She flung herself after him, each time rolling out of position or collapsing facedown with her legs all splayed. She ended on her back with her feet waving in the air. Wat pretended to try to get her up. She was immovable. He tugged and pushed and shoved. Nothing worked. It wasn't supposed to. Finally, feigning annoyance and defeat, he slouched off without a backward look. The bear scrambled to her feet and slouched after him.

When the Mirth Mongers applauded, Wat turned. The bear was taken aback by the sudden clapping and cheering. She stood stock-still, her head beginning to swing anxiously, one paw ripping at the muzzle. Wat ran to her with praise. He straightened the muzzle and pushed it up enough to allow her to open her mouth. He fed her some of Gunni's bread.

Kaila came, too. She spoke more bear words. She stayed with the cub, rubbing her and talking in a low voice. Meanwhile Dodder and the others discussed the show they would present and the money they would earn. Dodder explained to Wat that they had a special play to act. One scene was planned for the second night of the fair, another scene for the final evening. In between they would perform their tricks and dances and songs, and the bear could take part in these shows. She might even be used in one of the scenes. They would have to think some more and talk and practice together.

Wat was giddy with joy. Everything he had ever dreamed of seemed to be coming true. The Mirth Mongers treated him like one of the troupe. They included him in their plans. He was measured for a costume, slapped on the back, and spoken to by three people at the same time. It almost slipped his mind that without the bear cub they might not be so impressed. Nor did he consider what had brought Kaila and the bear and himself together with them. Three days! he thought, dazed and thrilled and so light-headed, he felt he could leap the frog with the bear standing upright. Three whole days to be one of the Mirth Mongers!

Later, leaving the cub in Kaila's care, he took the kettle back to Gunni and then went into the town in search of Brunn. The marketplace was lined with booths and stalls. And even around the green there were objects and services displayed, here a spice stall, there an iron monger with his bars of metal, and next to him a stall strung with poultry, and beside that the rat catcher with his sharp-eyed ferrets. Wat caught sight of the Lord's Steward sampling butter in tubs behind the butter booth. And here, gazing at a picture of a swollen-jawed fellow at the front of the tooth-drawer's booth, stood Brunn and Jennet. Brunn was shaking his head and rubbing his own cheek as Wat stepped between them.

They both exclaimed at once. Gunni had said he was gone for good. They had never expected to see him again.

"I came with the Mirth Mongers," Wat told them. He would have said more, but he remembered that this year their father had been made one of the Lord's Reeves.

"Can you juggle apples?" asked Jennet.

Wat shook his head. "Not yet."

Looking at the surcoat, Brunn remarked, "I can see you have not been digging clay or spreading cow dung in the fields."

Wat heard the edge to Brunn's tone. Coming back like this was not what Wat had imagined. "What has happened since I left?" he asked.

Brunn and Jennet exchanged a quick, uneasy glance. They strolled away from the tooth-drawer with him, as away as any could be now that the town hummed with last-minute preparations. "It has been hard," Brunn confided to Wat. "The Lord was ill for a long while. Then he was angry and looking for people to blame."

Wat thought he might learn more from Gunni, so he went back to the bake house.

Elbow-deep in dough, she knew his tread without even looking up. "Brushwood," she declared. "The ovens are cooling."

He stood watching her, wondering how to put his questions.

She glanced up. "Well? Make haste. How am I to keep the ovens going and the dough ready and the bread sold all at once? I must have flour, too."

Wat scurried out to the brushwood pile under the three-sided shed where the hens usually wintered.

"Time for one more haul of flour," she told him as he built up the oven fires. "Go to the mill. Quick, or the Lord's cook will take all the wheat meal Ulf has set aside for me."

Wat took off at a run. Once the fair was proclaimed, the gate would be closed and even the mill shut out. He saw horses ahead. Horses with saddles meant noblemen. He slowed. One of the men, astride a beautiful dapple-gray, was hurling insults and threats at the miller. Ulf was like an ox under the goad. He fetched two bags of flour and slowly set them before the man on the horse. He seemed unaware of the abuse heaped upon him.

"Where is the rest?" the horseman demanded. "The Lord will hear of it if his portion is short."

"These sacks are not his," Ulf answered.

"If not Havel's, whose?"

"Mine," Ulf replied. "And not for sale. If you take them, they must be considered a theft or a gift."

"The Lord of Urris needs no gift from the Odstone miller," the rider retorted. "These are his by right. The amount has increased this year because of the poor harvest."

The miller stood nearly as tall as the horse's upraised head, his massive arms folded across his chest. "A gift," he said quietly.

Another horseman said, "Oh, pay him, pay him. Haven't we enough quarrels with the town as it is?"

The man on the dapple-gray reached into his purse and flung some coins on the ground at the miller's feet. Bowing and turning his back on the horsemen, Ulf strode away, stepping on the money as he went. A servant hung the sacks on a packhorse; the horsemen started up the road to the gate. Wat watched them go, the rider on the beautiful gray horse still seething and vowing to return the miller's insult.

"They are desperate men," the miller told Wat afterward. "They know that the King is coming. They fear the reckoning." He went down into the dark place beneath the hopper where the wheels and shafts loomed like giant insect parts. Everything was fuzzy with mill dust and mysterious there, but the miller knew just where to find Gunni's sacks. He heaved two on each shoulder. "Have you the bear still?" he asked as they walked up the road together.

"She is with the Mirth Mongers behind the tailor."

Ulf of the Mill nodded thoughtfully. "They will have news, the

Mirth Mongers. We will go to them after I leave the flour with Gunni. I have an idea that I will spend the fair days inside Odstone, for news sifts down like meal from the corn. The town will be a turning stone. I am interested in what comes from that grinding."

What did Ulf mean? Wat supposed he would hear more when they came to Tailor's Close, but there was such a flurry of activity there that Wat lost track of Ulf. Nettle grabbed Wat and yanked him over to Bedstraw, who held something up behind him to measure, and pinched him in the process. Across the yard, Wat saw Ulf and Dodder coming out of the cow shed. Ulf had to stoop to clear the low doorway. Dodder walked upright, his trim and nimble body diminished beside the enormous miller, his short, tight-curled hair giving his bobbing head the look of a marsh marigold scarcely visible among thriving weeds. Yet for all the difference between them, they had the look of partners, like Spurge and Furze leaping and catching one another, like Kaila and the bear cub.

Dodder came forward to speak to him. "Spurge and Toadflax and I will follow the Steward and attend the proclamation of the fair. Everyone else will be at work here. Later we will all come together on the green. You and the bear will do your tumbling then. And tomorrow, in the morning, we must talk before you go into the fair. It would be wise," he added, "if you did not say much to the Reeve's children."

"Brunn and Jennet? They are my friends," Wat told him. "They have been since first I came to Odstone."

"And so they shall be when you leave it—if you avoid speaking with them."

Wat made no answer. He felt a heaviness inside him like a lump of raw dough.

But when the horn blared and all the town surged into the marketplace, Wat was caught up in the excitement. He found the town children, including Brunn and Jennet. All together, they joined the procession led by the Steward and the Lord's clerks and

Bailiff and Reeves. Behind them came a rider with the weights and measures, then a drover with a last flock of sheep scurrying to get inside the town before the gate was sealed.

Spurge and Toadflax and Dodder played and danced about the procession. There was a strange minstrel with a monkey on his shoulder. The Mirth Mongers kept edging him off the road and leaping in front of him to make him stumble. This was their fair, they seemed to be telling him, and when they arrived at the marketplace, it was they who piped the Steward and all the others to the odd stone.

There stood Clydog the Constable, about to pass on his white rod of power to the man who would be Chief Magistrate of the fair. Before this, there was a call for all vagabonds and idlers, all cheaters and rogues and beggars, to depart the town. No one stirred. No doubt the Fair Court would soon be hearing charges of robbery and cheating. But for now there was no outcry, no pointing fingers. Then the Steward called on all within the town to keep and uphold the King's peace. All fell silent. After a moment he shouted, "Let the gates be closed!"

Everyone saw the Constable hold out the white rod of office. Everyone saw the Lord's Bailiff urge his horse forward to take the rod from Clydog. But the way was clogged with townsfolk, and while the Bailiff kicked at his horse and swung at the heads of those blocking him, the massive figure of the miller could be seen cutting a swath through the crowd. People fell back to make way for him as he strode up to the odd stone. So it was Ulf standing tall upon his own two feet, not the Bailiff on his fine palfrey, who seized the white rod and swung it high, north and south.

"Let the Fair Court step forward," came his ringing command.

The Bailiff shouted something that was lost in the clamor, as men from every part of the town pressed close. Wat caught a glimpse of the tailor among them, of the cartwright and the blacksmith. For the next three days they would sit in judgment in the special court.

Something about this fair was different. Many of the townsfolk did not seem surprised that Ulf had taken the Bailiff's place. Wat could see the Bailiff conferring with the Steward. They could make no trouble for Ulf or the tailor and cartwright and black-smith and others. They could make no trouble for the next three days.

Later on, when Wat went to the bake house to take loaves into the marketplace, Gunni told him that in the old days the town had always chosen its Fair Court and Magistrate from among its own folk. But when he asked how it happened to come about this way now, she shook her head. "The less you know," she advised, "the less you can reveal."

"No one trusts anyone," he blurted.

Gunni fitted the carry strap to his tray. "It has been so for a while."

"Did you know that Ulf would—"

"Hush," she cautioned.

"But everyone knows."

Gunni frowned. "Then I will tell you this. The King has been sending messengers, but they have all been killed. He may not know that in this part of his kingdom he is challenged by the Lord of Urris. To this end, the Lord keeps us all on tight rein. He has offered me as wife to one of his Reeves from the east edge of the forest. He wants that Reeve in Odstone, for he will press the townsfolk hard. They will have to work still more to pay for bread, just as he intends that they will pay more at the mill for the corn they have grown on their own poor strips of land."

"When will you marry?" Wat asked, thinking that the bake house would never receive him again.

Gunni shoved him toward the door with his tray of bread. "Never," she declared.

Wat turned so sharply that several loaves slid to the floor. Stooping, Gunni picked them from the clean rushes and shook off bits of straw.

"You refused the Lord?"

Standing tall, she said, "I will marry the miller just as soon as we have the money to pay the Lord my bride price."

"Does the Lord know?"

"The Lord has been unwell," she remarked. "He avoids this town since he fell sick at the feast of the bear. His Steward comes in his stead. His Steward spares him disagreeable news. Now, will you sell my bread, or must I carry the tray myself?"

Wat nodded, but he was rooted to the spot. What she had said was just sinking in. She would be Ulf's wife.

Only she would not be free to marry until she could buy herself from Havel, Lord of Urris. That might take a very long time. Unless the King did come soon and they could reap the reward for the bear. Wat said, "If an ice bear is worth a king's ransom, then you will have your bride price and more before long."

Gunni frowned with puzzlement. "What are you saying? What has the bear to do with my bride price?"

Wat drew a long breath. He had counted on the royal reward for so long that he could not believe Gunni did not share that hope.

Gunni stepped closer. "Speak what is in your mind."

He resisted backing from her. If he did not stand his ground, how could he hold to his plan? "You yourself said it," he told her. "The King's bear. Will he not reward those who kept the last one safe for him?"

Gunni nodded slowly. "I see. I feared you might scheme that way. But the King is not yet here. The longer we keep the bear where Havel plots against the King and all he possesses, the less likely it is that the bear will live. Without the King and without the law of the kingdom, it is folly to live in expectation of justice or reward. I do not see riches attached to that bear. Do you know what I see? I see Kaila stolen from her homeland. The bear is all she has left of her people. That is what I see, not a bride price, not a king's ransom."

"Why do you care so?" he cried. "You have not wronged her."

Gunni did not answer at once. For a moment she was alone with her thoughts. Then she said, "I see beyond the bear and beyond Kaila to my mother. Her grief and longing were in every tale of Firland, in every song. I was only a child then. But now . . ." Gunni spread her hands wide. "Now there is Kaila, and I am a child no longer. Can you understand what I feel?"

Wat nodded grudgingly and then set off with the bread. Maybe when he had time to reflect, the understanding would come. Not now, though. He paused at the edge of the green to watch the men who challenged one another at single-stick. In a while he would take his place on the green, too. What if the bear refused to play? Just thinking about it made his stomach tighten, as if it were caught in a snare.

He walked about with his hands raised to fend off those who would snatch a loaf without paying. He caught sight of the minstrel with the monkey in front of a stall where whetstones were sold. Whetstones! No household in Odstone was allowed its own whetstone. All the hooks and knives and scythes were brought to the Reeve and sharpened at a price. But here stood ordinary townsfolk selecting whetstones for their own use. They would sharpen what they liked now, including tools like fire pikes that could be used as weapons as well. Feeling the minstrel's eyes upon him, Wat moved on into the crowd.

12

Wat was drawn to the herbalist's stall. Some of the maimed and afflicted, too poor to pay for salves of ground beetles that could draw the pain from a crooked leg or a wrist stump, offered the herbalist leeks and earthenware pots and salted ox flesh. He looked with interest at Wat's bread and held up a dragon tooth as enticement. Sweeping the tooth back and forth, he extolled its virtues and assured one and all that it cured every kind of falling sickness. Wat was tempted. Surely something as wonderful and ancient held other powers as well. The tooth was perfectly curved and very white.

Feeling a tug from behind, Wat turned. There was Little Robin, dressed like a small fool in a tunic of many colors.

"You are to come at once," the child said.

Turning reluctantly from the dragon tooth, Wat said he must first return the bread tray to the bake house.

"You go to the tailor's," said Little Robin. "I will take the tray."

Wat had to laugh as the small boy made off with it, his head thrust forward like a tiny ox bearing a heavy load.

Behind the tailor's house the troupe was transformed. Furze was a straw bear, Spurge his leader. Dodder wore scraps of leather, a tail, and long floppy ears. There was a similar costume for Wat, but Kaila wore a motley tunic like Little Robin's and a mask to conceal her face.

The Mirth Mongers had been making many masks; they were lined up on the thatch of the cow shed to dry. Wat wanted to look at them all, but there was no time to spare.

They set off in a procession led by pipes and tabor. The straw bear danced and occasionally lunged at a bystander. Little Robin raced from side to side with a basket into which he had put stones and bits of metal that clinked invitingly. Wat would have liked to turn cartwheels to make the bells jingle at his knees and wrists, but he didn't dare leave Kaila and the bear. She walked as though made of wood. Wat kept up a stream of talking to remind Kaila how important it was for her to make the bear cub behave.

"Did you hear me?" he demanded when she forged straight on as though sleepwalking.

She turned to him for a moment, her masked face grinning.

In the late-afternoon sun the odd stone cast a deeply slanting shadow, jagged and broken by steps and people in its path. Just as the Mirth Mongers stepped onto the green, so did the solitary minstrel. Dodder bowed to him. He challenged the intruder to best them at any of their exploits. Bedstraw and Nettle were already juggling. People gasped when the jugglers shared each other's balls. Before they finished, Toadflax set down his pipe and began a series of flip-flaps. As the audience cheered and shouted, Furze, dressed as the straw bear, tried to mimic him. The crowd laughed and clapped.

"Now!" said Dodder, giving Wat a shove.

Wat glanced back at the bear and Kaila. He felt another push and ran onto the grass. The bear followed, but haltingly. Wat began his somersaults, but the bear only stood with her head low and slightly turned from the people who watched. The straw bear took the real bear's place and mimicked Wat. There was laughter. Wat saw the bear start to swing her head. "Speak to her," he called to Kaila. "Make her work."

Kaila spoke, and the bear crouched stiffly. She did not fold her paws inward at her chest. Her claws were spread as if to clutch the ground.

Wat vaulted over her and then somersaulted across her back. The crowd thought that was grand, but the bear showed no signs of playfulness. Jumping astride her, Wat told Kaila to lead her in a circle. Carefully he rose to his feet. The audience roared its approval. Wat needed something more to keep the performance from collapsing. He glanced around. There was Little Robin in his many-colored tunic. Wat called him to the bear, dropped down onto the bear's back, and reached for the child. Little Robin came dancing to him. A deep growl vibrated through the bear as Wat snatched the child up. He told Little Robin to mount his shoulders. Pulling himself to his knees and gripping the thick fur with one hand, Wat steadied Little Robin with the other and rose, trembling, his own feet slipping partway down the bear's sides. With his legs bowed, he straightened his upper body and extended his arms. The bear walked on with Kaila. Wat waited the length of a few good breaths before he raised his hands, grabbed the child, and leapt backward with Little Robin clutched to him.

As he landed with Little Robin safely behind the bear, Mirth Mongers took his place on the green. There followed one of their marvelous tumbling acts that drew shouts and cries from the crowd. Little Robin ran among the audience with his basket. Wat just stood there, his heart still hammering, grateful that he had no more to do.

The solitary minstrel set up a rope on two supports; his monkey danced on it and swung around and around. Dodder beckoned the minstrel and called for the bear. Full of misgiving, Wat listened to Dodder challenge the minstrel, who slowly approached the bear. Her lips curled back in a snarl. The audience howled, egging on the minstrel and the bear.

No more, Wat willed. Oh, no more. At any moment now this game would turn into bear-baiting and bloodshed.

The Mirth Mongers taunted the minstrel. Dodder told Wat to act the fool with the bear. "Show everyone how you give the beast a bear hug."

"I've shown enough," Wat protested. "Let Kaila take the bear away."

All around them, people—men and women and children from the town, merchants from afar, the low and the highborn—pressed forward with eager babbling. The only hope Wat had was to make them quiet. Falling deliberately on top of Dodder, Wat pleaded and explained all at once. Dodder picked himself up and waved for attention. Gradually the throng fell silent.

"If you are very still," Dodder told them, "you will hear the ancient language of dragons spoken. But you must be absolutely quiet."

Meanwhile Wat, his voice low, said to Kaila, "The cub is in danger. If you play, so will she. Otherwise they may come with sticks." How much threat could Kaila stand? "They will come with sticks to poke the bear, to make her angry. If she hurts someone . . ." If only he could see Kaila's face. "You must speak to her," he directed shakily.

"How?" she asked miserably, as if she hadn't a thought of her own.

"Loud. Make the bear do something. Anything."

Kaila shouted a command in her own bear language. The bear stood up on her hind legs. Kaila shouted another bear word. The cub, unused to the shouting, hesitated before slowly revolving. The crowd applauded.

Dodder announced, "This ancient language comes from a time when all the wild beasts spoke with one voice. That is the dragon speech of old. Few people can hear the bear's reply, but the little fool who speaks with her can hear it if you all remain silent."

Wat sighed with relief. Not only had Dodder taken hold of Wat's notion, but he had gone far beyond anything Wat could have devised. Next the bear lay on her back, her paws waving, quite unlike the vicious-looking animal of before. Wat took his place with her then. Straddling the cub, he placed first one sweaty hand, then the other, against the pads of the bear's forepaws. He had to remind himself not to grab hold, for that would bring her claws against his fingers. Flat-palmed, he leaned forward. Now

came the first leg. Then the other. "All right," he whispered to
Kaila. She spoke again, no longer shouting, for there wasn't a
sound on all the green. The bear stiffened, supporting Wat. Very
easily and gently she began to rock on her curved back with Wat
suspended over her. She brought her head up higher, until her
snout touched Wat's forehead. She tried to lick him, but the muzzle interfered. It was a good moment to end. He bent his legs. He
could feel hers propel him as he sprang free of her.

"You have heard bear talk that is akin to the speech of dragons,"
Dodder informed the crowd. "You have seen a bear who speaks in
the ancient tongue that only a few humans can understand. You
may cheer."

Through the tumult the Mirth Mongers prepared to depart.
Wat was in a daze, steaming and breathless, exultant and still
shaken with terror. Full of rapture, he grabbed up Little Robin
and set him on the bear cub. There was a delicious aroma of an ox
roasting. There were other smells, like garlic and ale. They cleared
Wat's head a little. Suddenly he was intensely hungry, intensely
happy.

When Little Robin waved to the crowd, Wat said to Kaila,
walking on the other side of the bear, "You wave, too. It can't
hurt you to wave."

She cast him a look that he couldn't read through her mask, but
her shoulders told him she was spent. This was his play, she
seemed to be saying, his triumph. It was enough for her that she
and the bear had endured.

When all the Mirth Mongers were gathered at Tailor's Close,
Wat learned that for the second day of the fair Dodder planned to
act out the bear hanging and the Feast of Fools. Aghast, Wat
asked why.

"Because," said Dodder, "somewhere in this throng is a messenger for the King. If we replay the hanging and turn the bear feast
into the Feast of Fools, all the townsfolk will speak of those events
and the messenger will learn what he needs to know. And he is

certain to attend our show, for he knows that we Mirth Mongers go where few are allowed—and leave again. If you join us, you will learn that as we travel from town to town and manor to manor, we never fail to sing the praises of the mighty, though often in a mocking way to reveal some hidden truths."

Wat heard very little after the words *If you join us.* He went to Kaila and said, "We might go south with the Mirth Mongers," but she didn't seem to grasp what he told her. She wanted him to show her the road to the north. She made the cub stay in the cow shed and followed him to the sealed gate.

"From here," he warned, "the way is wild and full of danger."

"How many days to the sea?"

He had no idea. He said, "If we go with the Mirth Mongers, we might reach another sea. We will have money to go away."

"North," she told him. "Home."

He tried to explain that if she went this way, she might be delivering the bear to another captivity or death. And herself as well. She did not answer him. Good, he thought. She must be considering his warning. She would come to her senses.

They returned in silence to Tailor's Close. The Mirth Mongers were already rehearsing tomorrow's play. Kaila stopped in her tracks when she realized that there was to be a mock hanging of the bear.

"It is pretend," Wat told her.

Still she did not move.

"To make people laugh at the fools who feasted on the heart of the she-bear. You remember."

"No one laughed," she reminded him.

"They did not know what was happening," Dodder explained. "We will play it out to give them the understanding." He scooped up a handful of pebbles, then dropped them in a little heap. "Look," he said as he sorted the gray ones from the pink ones and set the blackest ones at his knee. In a flash his fingers pushed some and arranged others. And there, with the black at the center, was a flower. "Out of the jumble comes a picture . . . so. When we take an event and act it out, we do the same. Tomorrow we will show Odstone folk that the Feast of Fools they all know from stories and merrymaking really happened before their eyes. They will begin to think about that. And on the last day, when we dance and play the harvest game of the straw man, we will show them how the end of one story may be the beginning of another. When they are stirred by the story, they will begin to resist the Lord of Misrule. The King's messenger will mark it all."

Kaila fixed her troubled gaze on Dodder. "What will happen to the bear cub?"

Dodder threw up his hands. "Nothing. Nothing at all."

"She will be dead, and you will cut out her heart for the Feast of Fools."

"Oh, Kaila," cried Wat in exasperation, "you have not listened to a word."

Dodder scowled at him. "Only in play," he said gently. "We will only *seem* to hang her. Then she must drop. Then we will make a great show of cutting out her heart. A show, child, not really doing it." He could see Kaila's disbelief. "Listen. Every year at this time men and women thrash the grain from the stalks. Every year we play the straw man. This year we will all thrash Furze to the ground, but he will not be hurt. It is true, but it is not real."

Kaila looked horrified. "Why?" she whispered. "What is it for?"

"For the harvest. For the end of growing and the season of cold and death. Every year we cut down the grain; we thrash the straw man with our flails."

"And then," put in Wat excitedly, "then up he gets. Under the straw he is green. That means the corn will grow again. We see it every year."

Kaila slowly shook her head. "Where is my father, then? Where is the she-bear and the other cub? They do not get up again. Where is my mother?"

Wat threw Dodder a beseeching look.

Dodder did not speak for a while. Finally he said, "That is the truth, too, and we will show that. Yes," he went on, nodding to himself, "it is how we will play the scene."

"You have not told me," said Kaila.

"I will," Dodder replied. "I will tell you in our dance and play. You will see part of it tomorrow and the rest of it at our last play. And you must help us to tell the story. When you do that, you will be telling the story of your mother and father and the bear, and many others as well."

"And you will give me an answer?" Kaila asked him.

"You will have your answer," Dodder promised.

Something in his manner was so convincing that she went about her practice with the bear as though she had never had a doubt or misgiving. But Wat noticed that Dodder took no chances with her. It was Wat who was to take her part and stand in the midst of the revels facing the fools at their feast. It seemed a paltry part to play, but Wat knew better than to raise any objections.

As Dodder worked out everyone's actions, Toadflax composed one verse after another telling of the heroic deeds of the Lord of Urris. And while Toadflax walked about the tailor's yard muttering to himself, Dodder and Nettle instructed Wat in the order of events and made him repeat what he must do. Nothing must go awry, they said. Everything and everyone in place.

Little Robin wanted to know when he should climb onto the bear's back.

"Not climb," Wat hastened to warn him. "Someone will put you there."

"You climb. You play with the bear."

"She knows me," Wat explained.

"Soon she will know me, too. When we travel together."

Wat nodded but said nothing.

"What name will you take for the road?"

"I am Wat. It is my name wherever I go."

"We are named for the wayside weeds," the little boy told him.

Spurge said, "That is so, for we are in and out of every town and manor house without question. It is only as Mirth Mongers that we are known."

Wat liked the idea of a name for the road. He dropped his voice so that Kaila would not overhear him. "What weeds are there?" he asked.

Teasel declared with a sly look, "I know just the one for you: Fleabane!"

"How about the one called Mind Your Own Business," retorted Spurge.

Wat laughed. He said it might suit Kaila better. But he doubted she would answer to another name.

"Then we will call her Sea Kale. She can scarcely mind that."

Dodder cut in. They could consider road names later. There was work for all, and not much time to learn the changes for the Feast of Fools.

As the Mirth Mongers planned and practiced, Wat marveled at how swiftly they took on other people's features. Dodder most of all. His face was drawn as he stepped into his scene. In an instant he gained a heavy chin and a portly swagger. His mouth was greedy, his eyes cunning. Wat had to wrench himself away. There was the cow shed to clean out before nightfall.

13

The bear led the procession to draw attention away from the Mirth Mongers lugging props and masks and cloth for the play. Only Bedstraw walked with Wat and Kaila to keep an eye on Little Robin, who sat astride the bear waving wildly.

Scanning the throng for familiar faces, Wat caught sight of the solitary minstrel. The next time he glanced that way, the minstrel had disappeared. Wat quickened his step. The bear was moving easily. She seemed less bothered by the crowds this afternoon.

For one instant Wat saw her as she must look to the people. She had something of the swagger of the she-bear now. Her shoulders jutted high and flexible as she strode along. With her head carried low, her ears flattened, she might seem menacing to those who had seen the she-bear swiping out with savage lunges. Yet here sat Little Robin, a perfect fool for being utterly fearless. Wat let the bear cub sniff his hand before he plunged it into the thick neck fur. He scrubbed with his fingertips and felt her press against him with pleasure. They walked that way onto the green. Then he lifted Little Robin down and sent him running to Bedstraw.

Wat began his tumbling. The bear, in sloppy pursuit, fell all over herself. Laughter came from every side. Wat invented games as he went along, with the bear copying everything. They ended with leap-the-frog, Wat first and the bear following with surprising agility. There were gasps as Wat crouched and covered his head with his arms. The bear hurtled over him. When she landed, she crouched, too, her own forelegs wrapped around her head as though she feared Wat's next leap. The crowd could see that she was clowning. They called for another leap and another. By the time Dodder and Toadflax and Spurge came forward with music and juggling, Wat's ears were ringing and he hadn't enough breath to speak to the bear. He just leaned against her as they walked to the side.

Brunn and Jennet ran to him. They were thrilled and envious. But wasn't it the King's bear?

Wat said, "This bear is a visitor from the north. She has human understanding. Do you think an ordinary bear could speak and do what she does?"

"I could not hear what she said," Brunn told him.

"That is because it is the bear language."

Jennet said "Oh!" with a quick intake of breath, but Brunn looked doubtful.

"This is a warrior bear," Wat went on. "A whole troop of horse-men armed with lances and swords could not best it in battle."

Brunn was silenced for a moment. Then he asked, "How do you know?"

Wat told him recklessly, "It is well known in the world beyond. We who travel from town to town and manor to manor and fair to fair, we learn such things. Its fame is like a hero's deeds." He saw that others had gathered and were listening. One day, he thought, he might become a chanter of tales, but just now it seemed important to say no more. He thought he glimpsed the minstrel again and quickly looked away. He did not want a challenge from a man well versed in song and story.

"Make haste," called Bedstraw, rescuing him. "Dodder says make haste."

The Mirth Mongers had completed the entertainment on the green and were arranging themselves for the Feast of Fools. While Wat had cavorted with the bear and drawn all eyes to the sport, Dodder and the others had set a board on trestles where the Lord and his company had supped on meat and bread and honey and bear.

Bedstraw pushed Wat toward the table, but he faltered when he saw Kaila and the bear approaching the gallows. Did Kaila realize what the Mirth Mongers were miming as they tossed the noose over the bear's head? Dodder, cloaked in black and with black cloth covering all his face but his eyes, spoke to Kaila, who in turn spoke to the bear. The cub rose until she was standing to her full height, much taller than Dodder.

All the fair drew close. By now darkness was descending with autumn swiftness. Spurge tapped the tabor and chanted a tale about an absent king who entrusted his realm to his lords. Words were fused with sounds, words like *loath* and *Lythe,* like *sneer* and *snare* and *snarl.* The rhythm and sounds trapped the mind, made it captive to certain phrases that remained even after Spurge went on.

The people stood rapt and silent. They swayed slightly as the chant carried them off to the royal forest where none might chase the King's game but those permitted by royal decree. A great white bear, a monarch from the Land of the White Falcons, hunted there at the King's pleasure. But not alone—oh, not alone. For a certain lord with a mighty hunger, a consuming hunger for more than royal game, gave chase in the crownland, gave refuge to robbers and cutthroats, and seized the white monarch, the ice bear.

Someone shouted from the ranks of listeners. Others hushed him.

"Here now," chanted Spurge, "come your Men of Law, your defenders of the King's peace."

Toadflax stepped to the table. He was wearing a donkey-head mask with huge flopping ears and a mouth stretched wide.

"Hear them utter their solemn judgment," Spurge continued as Toadflax brayed loudly. The crowd roared with delight. Meanwhile Teasel joined the donkey Man of Law. His head was black and beaked. He delivered a harsh, rude screech, so that Wat knew, along with everyone else, that here was the bird of death, the raven.

In the gloom, the black-hooded Dodder raised his arms and whipped the rope taut. Wat lurched at that. The crowd gasped as with a single breath. Wat saw mouths gaping, eyes wide and staring. They were no different from that other time when they cried for blood and strained for a clear view of it. Where were those who knew this was not real? Wat caught sight of Bedstraw, her arm about Kaila. But where were the others? Spurge's chanting fell away. Everything was gone but a kind of buzzing in Wat's ears. He tried to push through to the gallows. He tried to shout. He felt as though he were inside an enormous hive. His voice came out a squeak as the bear whipped around and seemed to leave the ground.

He flung himself, hive and all, toward the scaffold. His hands were flailing, as if at swarms of bees that blurred his vision and stopped his breath. Then he broke through. There was the bear, lying flat, Kaila kneeling beside her. He felt Dodder gripping his shoulder, but he wrenched it free and cast himself on the bear.

"Leave that to the girl," Dodder instructed. "We must move on to the feast."

Someone was playing music and singing. The bear lay inert. Kaila was still. With a cry of fury, Wat lunged at Dodder but missed him. Kaila gazed at Wat through her mask. "You are to be with the dancers," she told him. "I am to stay with the bear."

He stared at her, uncomprehending. Then he felt the great furred body stir. The cub was rubbing her shoulder against the hard edge of the odd stone.

Wat rocked back. He had to clutch her fur to keep from losing his balance. He felt so drained and weak and simple, that was all he could do, hold on to her.

He was slow to come back to the show. Here and there torches were lit. Wat looked over to the table and saw that Nettle had taken a place there. She looked strangely elegant in a lady's gown. Dodder, still in black, made his way to the seat of honor. The raven hopped upon the table and snatched something from the lady, then darted back to his place. Released from the tension of the gallows scene, the crowd began to laugh. The dancers performing for the feast threw themselves about with drunken abandon. Wat moved toward his position, but he could not act his part, not yet. He felt such a fool now. Maybe the onlookers assumed that his distress was part of the mime, but how could he face the Mirth Mongers?

He watched the hooded and robed Dodder conduct the Steward to the trestle table. Only it wasn't the Steward; it was Toadflax. And now came Ulf. It had to be the real Ulf, for no one else was that size. Ulf removed his hood to reveal straw hair and four long straw braids. Everyone knew at once that he must be the Lord's daughter. They roared at the ridiculous sight of the huge miller playing the part of the maiden.

In the midst of the hilarity Dodder, with one sweep of his arm, threw off the black hood and cloak. All the laughter broke off. There stood Dodder in murrey cloth, the Lord's color, and with a head of false hair parted in the middle and falling in tight tiers of ringlets. The crowd made a sound like a winter wind. Dodder bowed to the right and to the left, his slight stature as ill-fitting for the Lord as Ulf in the guise of maiden. But as soon as Dodder clapped his hands for food, he took on the Lord's manner. Real food was brought, ale and cakes and a joint of ox.

The bear's nose twitched as she picked up the scent of meat. Kaila leaned over her and spoke a single word of warning. Lord Dodder slapped the joint aside and pounded the table, upsetting a cup of ale into maiden Ulf's lap. At that, the maiden leapt to her feet in mock dismay, showing to all the roaring throng her spoiled gown, which she raised up immodestly. That brought thunderous applause. It brought Wat into his place as well. If Ulf could act the fool like that, then surely Wat could set aside his shame and take his part.

Lord Dodder thrust out his arms in a commanding gesture. Everyone knew that he called for the heart of the ice bear. There was no chanting now, only the story in action and dance. Here came Nettle to lean over the bear, now on her back and still playing dead. Nettle made a great show of carving out the heart and carrying it to the table. This was fare fit for noblemen and lords, who made an even greater show of gobbling what was placed before them. The joint of ox became the heart, the Lord and his Steward squabbling over it. At length the Lord snatched it to his murrey chest and, with a snarl, satisfied his bestial greed.

Now Spurge took up the chant again. He repeated the phrases about the Lord's consuming hunger for a bear's heart and a King's realm. "Let the mighty eat of the mighty bear that they gain in courage and strength. The heart of the bear makes a fool's feast. See how they rise up as though the thing they ate of did grow inside them. Grow and grow until they would seem to burst from it."

By now those who played the noblemen were casting themselves about in agony or making a great display of staggering off to be sick upon the ground.

"Take the bear to them," Nettle said. She was dancing behind Wat. She could feel the crowd surge forward before he did. Everyone around him was shouting insults and grievances. A few of the townsfolk even hurled themselves on the fools, kicking and walloping, clearly forgetting they were really Mirth Mongers. Ulf had to roar the people down to restore enough order to let the Mirth Mongers depart.

"The players beg your leave," Spurge shouted, "and ask your consideration for our final play."

Some who heard him made room for Wat and Kaila and the bear. Spurge leapt on the table and shook the tabor hard. "See who lies weak as a nestling," he chanted, pointing to the Lord of Misrule, who lay writhing on the ground. An unrehearsed dog ambled over to sniff him, and laughter overcame the angry voices. Kaila had already tied a length of rawhide across the bear's chest and around her middle. Wat tied Dodder's feet to the circlet, and the bear lumbered out of the marketplace with the Lord of Misrule dragging behind her.

Wat missed the final words that Spurge chanted. They seemed to hold the crowd in check, but Dodder remarked as Wat unhitched him that it would be well to avoid the fair through the rest of the night. There was no telling how far folk might go, with their bellies full of ale and their heads ajumble with the sight of the Lord being dragged through the dirt by the King's bear.

Dodder was right. Sounds of turmoil from the green and marketplace made sleep impossible at Tailor's Close. Only Kaila and the bear, allowed back inside the cleaned cow shed, had any proper rest.

By dawn the Mirth Mongers were at work again, each a tailor and a mask-maker. They sat in a close circle, their heads bent over their handwork and their low voices setting out the scene and action for their last mime.

Wat, who was supposed to be attaching sticks to resemble flails, stopped for a moment, his hands clutching his ears. That stilled the buzzing that had started up again inside his head.

"Maybe our young friend should take himself inside the shed and sleep awhile," Dodder suggested.

Wat dropped his hands to his knees. Shaking his head, he picked up two sticks and tied them end to end. He heard Dodder speaking about him.

"If we are traveling with an ice bear," Dodder declared, "our fame will follow us and, in time, precede us. It is a risk."

Bedstraw said, "But we knew when you dressed yourself as a straw bear that we intended to show the Lord of Misrule. And that was before Wat and the girl and the bear joined us."

Dodder nodded. "That is true. But it is important that each of you understand the risk." He turned to Wat. "It is decided, then. We will have you as one of us, if you choose to come our way. But we must have your decision soon, for it matters how and when we depart from here. No one else can know what we plan, for we do not know who might betray us." Dodder sighed. "How alike we become in distrust. Havel stayed from the fair because of the danger that surrounds him where his power is keenly felt. I hear that he suspects this one and that one in his service. No doubt he has some person here watching and listening for him, just as the King has his messenger."

"You think it is the minstrel who listens and watches for the Lord of Urris," said Spurge.

Dodder shrugged. "He may be the one. I do not think him apt in his art, and he avoids all contests with us. There is something false about him, the way he is both bold and timid. And always there."

Wat thought, yes, that solitary minstrel was never far from any unusual occurrence.

"And what do you say to our invitation?" Dodder prompted him.

Wat gave a sigh.

"So hard a decision?"

"Would you consider traveling north?" Wat pleaded. "There are fishing villages along the coast. Surely they would pay you well. You would be a rare sight for them."

Dodder shook his head. "The road north is full of dangers even when the days are long and the weather fair. How could we prevail against wild men and outlaws? Our only weapons are the barbs of our tongues. No rogue charging down the mountains would bother to give us a hearing. We would not live long by our wits that way."

Wat stared bleakly at him.

Dodder added, "The road south branches at the river. There is a way over the bridge that takes us west out of Urris lands to yet another crossroad, with more choices after that. But whichever way we take, the winter will be the milder and the great houses warmer with welcome than any in Urris or north of here."

Wat could not refuse the Mirth Mongers. He must not. "It is the bear and the girl," he said.

"You will convince her if you set yourself to it," Teasel insisted. "Do not look so downhearted. You must win her over with joy."

"Yes," agreed Spurge. "Joy. And there's your name for you. Traveler's Joy."

"What?" said Wat through an enormous yawn.

"Traveler's Joy. A roadside weed. You see its flower twisted among branches and bushes, sprays of white caught up in growing things."

Wat nodded. He could barely keep his eyes open. He managed a smile to show them his pleasure at the prospect of becoming a Mirth Monger. His joy.

Little Robin came stumbling into their midst, rubbing his eyes. Bedstraw opened her arms to him, and he nestled against her. Dodder smiled at them, and then looked grave, his mind taken up with the departure.

"Is there no other way out but through the gate?" he asked Wat. "You know the town better than we do."

Wat did not think that any opening remained. "They finished the wall while I was away," he answered, "but I could ask Brunn—"

"Your friend whose father is Reeve?"

Wat nodded.

"Say nothing to him," warned Dodder. "Get your sleep now, and put your mind to the question when you are rested." Then a fresh idea seemed to come to him, because he stopped short and clapped his hand to his forehead. "We must leave before the peace ends and the gates are opened. There is no apparent way to do this; yet there is one at least for whom the gate would open." All in the circle tensed. Sewing hands upraised, everyone still. Dodder nodded to himself. "The King's messenger carries a Writ of Safe Conduct under the royal signet. For him the gate would open."

"If the King's messenger reveals himself," murmured Bedstraw, "he will be parted from the King's signet before we know it."

Dodder rubbed his bristly head. "I know, I know. But it means there is a way to leave in advance of the others. We must look for that way." He nodded at Wat. "Get to your rest," he directed. "You will need your wits about you, and your strength."

Wat staggered into the cow shed. The rank smell of bear assailed him in the close darkness. He dropped to his knees on a bundle of straw. Nearly asleep, he had to twist around to keep the pouch from digging into his ribs. Later, when he waked briefly, his fingers tingled where it pressed against his hand. Dodder, he thought as he flexed his fingers. Something for Dodder. When he got up, he would be able to think what it was he must do for Dodder. When he had his wits about him.

14

Late in the day Wat broke his fast with fresh barley bread, green cheese, and watered ale. Stretching out beside him, the bear extended one fat paw. Hardly thinking, Wat slapped it aside. The bear groaned, sidled closer, and batted his arm. He jumped up. There would be no peace until she was fed. Rummaging through the skin bags, he pulled out some strips of dried meat. The cub sat up then, her hind legs straight out in front of her, and ate along with him in companionable silence.

All around the yard Mirth Mongers were lying asleep. Dodder had rolled himself inside the murrey cloth. One of the tailor's hens came up to him, pecking hopefully at his head of yellow curls. He snorted in his sleep and drew his head under the purple cover. When he awoke, Wat would give him the royal Writ. It was only right that Dodder carry it. As leader of the troupe, he would show it to the porter at the gate. They would be away before anyone knew it.

Wat glanced up at the leaden sky. The sun was nothing more than a dirty greenish stain. With so little daylight left, Wat was eager to go into the marketplace one last time. When Kaila walked into the yard, he turned on her. "Where have you been?" he cried. "This is the last day. Don't you know there is much to be done?"

She was carrying what looked like an empty sack. She opened and upended it onto the ground. Out poured coins, many coins.

He gasped. What had she been up to?

She reached under a fold of her tunic to show him a sheathed knife. "The blade is not as fine as yours, but now at least we each have one."

He swept his hand over the coin-littered ground. "Where does all this come from?"

"The skins," she said. "Gunni told me how to sell them." Then she added, "I kept skins for sleeping under, and one of the badger to finish your leggings with. You will have them in your pack in a while."

Something troubled him about her preparations. Did she understand the arrangements made during the night? He said, "We must go with the Mirth Mongers, you know."

She listened to him, her eyes unwavering.

"Do you understand what I am saying?"

She nodded.

Relieved, he talked about the money they would earn and the warm houses and halls that would be open to them over the bitter nights ahead. They might find themselves performing before greater lords than Havel. Someday they might even play before the King himself. And all the while they would have protection and companionship and joy.

She eyed him levelly, without saying a word.

It suddenly occurred to Wat that Dodder must have been speaking to Gunni to prepare the way for convincing Kaila. Everything had been accomplished while Wat slept, even the fetching of fresh-baked barley bread for their breakfast. Gunni must have persuaded Kaila when she advised her about selling the skins. He was glad the persuading had not been left to him.

Wat divided up the coins. That way, if one of them was robbed, they would still have some on hand.

"You have the other," Kaila reminded him. "In the pouch."

"I know," he answered. "It may be needed here. We may not carry it all away with us."

Kaila did not ask him why. She was more concerned with finishing his leggings than worrying about the treasures in his pouch.

When he asked her to make a pigskin ball for the bear, she put it together hastily, stuffed it with straw, stitched it up, and paid no further attention to him.

At first the bear refused to share the ball with him. Wat almost gave up. He was about to go on to the marketplace when Dodder sat up and said, "Throw the ball to me." Wat threw and Dodder caught. They tossed it back and forth while the bear's head swiveled to watch. "To her!" Dodder shouted as he jumped to his feet and backed off. Wat threw the ball to the bear, who caught it and clutched it to her chest. "We should turn our backs," Wat told Dodder, for that was a sign of displeasure to the bear.

Both Wat and Dodder stood with their backs presented to the bear.

"Don't move," cautioned Bedstraw softly. "She is thinking it over."

Wat suddenly called, "Fish!" He wheeled just in time to catch the ball as the bear slung it to him. He tossed it right back. Dodder turned, too, and held out his arms, but the bear threw the ball at Wat again. They went on from there, Dodder pretending to try to intercept the ball, Wat and the bear thwarting every attempt. They played like that until Dodder was called away to the tailor's house. Breathless with laughter and joy, Wat set aside the ball, waited awhile, and then went off to wander through the fair.

Fingering the coins, he approached the booth where the dragon tooth was displayed. The herbalist was applying a split frog to the bloodied forehead of a young man injured in a contest of single-stick. When the young man asked for water to wash the blood from his face and hands, the cost of the treatment rose accordingly. Then it was Wat's turn.

"The dragon tooth," he said. "May I look at it?"

"Let you hand me the money and then look."

"Is it more than a loaf of wheaten bread?"

The herbalist snorted. "It is worth three wheaten loaves."

Aghast, his hand poised to receive the tooth, Wat hesitated.

An onlooker said, "If you overprice the thing, the Fair Court will hear of it. You will forfeit the price."

Glowering, the herbalist declared, "Two wheaten loaves."

Wat, who had never bought anything before, craved the tooth. Carefully he counted out the coins.

"Now," declared another onlooker, "you have your payment. Give the lad the tooth."

The next moment it lay in Wat's hand. It felt smooth and worn with age and power. Wat was thrilled.

Hurrying back to Tailor's Close, Wat extracted the royal Writ from his pouch. He found Dodder and Kaila locked in a quiet, but intense, disagreement. Wat called out, "I have something important for you!" At the same time Dodder swung around and said, "Explain to the girl why we cannot travel with a beast that might lop off the head of a patron or eat one of his children."

Wat stopped short. "You do not want the bear?"

"Of course we do. We must break her eyeteeth, that is all."

Wat's heart skipped a beat. He could feel the heat rising straight up to the roots of his hair. "But she is perfect!" he blurted. "I mean, she is only a cub."

Dodder spread his hands wide. The necessity was so clear, he seemed to be saying, that it needed no further explanation.

Kaila ducked inside the cow shed.

Then Dodder spoke again. "It is best done in a town. We need strong arms to hold the bear. To pry open the mouth. The black-smith can knock out the teeth." Sensing Wat's resistance, Dodder suddenly changed the subject. "What important thing did you bring?"

Wat was holding the wooden slabs. Now he untied the cord and pulled the parchment out. Dodder examined it. He seemed afraid to believe what he saw.

"I read a little," he said finally. "But sometimes I read what I wish in the writing."

"It is a Writ of Safe Conduct," Wat told him. "That is the

King's signet." He went on to tell Dodder how he came to carry it.

"You had it all this while?" Dodder exclaimed.

Kaila came out of the shed leading the bear. Without a word or a backward glance, she headed downhill.

Wat said to Dodder, "I didn't know what use could be made of it. Until you spoke. Then I knew it was for all of us. For leaving."

Dodder closed his hands over it and nodded. Wat heaved a sigh. He felt as though the Writ bound him more closely to the Mirth Mongers. But anxiety over Kaila mingled with his relief. He would go after her now. He would tell her that what must be done to the bear was for all of them. Like the Writ.

He guessed that she had gone to the bake house, but when he got there, he found that the great floury bearprints led away from the door. Inside, Gunni straightened slowly and said, "The bear cannot hunt without her teeth. Kaila knows that if the teeth are broken, the bear will be captive always. And herself as well."

Wat flushed. It was true that he had not thought beyond the coming winter with the Mirth Mongers.

Gunni said, "You will lose her."

He felt a sudden onrush of anger. Why did Gunni always catch him up in conflict? Watching her dump a new batch of dough onto her floured board, he realized she would never yield ground to him if she thought him wrong. He was reminded of the bird-man choosing to remain where he could serve his King and restore his good name. If ever he could recall it.

Gunni raised the dough and slapped it down again and again. She would not look at him.

Wat reached into his pouch for the second time that afternoon. He drew out one of the large coins. "How much to buy your freedom?" he asked her.

Now she looked. At his hand. The powerful arms remained up-lifted, the dough slowly falling onto the board. "What do you mean?"

"So that you and Ulf can marry."

She faced him. "What have you done?"

"There are more coins like this one. I had thought to pay for passage to the Islands of Tor and Firland and beyond."

"Then keep them for that."

"There will be enough. We are taking money at this fair, and there will be more as we go along. So what must you have to make up the bride price? Is this what you need?" he asked, fetching out more of the smaller coins and another large one. "I have been told that the big ones are worth a great deal."

Dusting her floury hands, Gunni picked one large coin and several small ones from his open palm. Then she closed his fingers over the remaining coins. "This is almost the amount," she told him.

"Take more," he pleaded. It seemed to him that if she had it all, then she might let him go.

"It is what we need," she said. "And it leaves you with what you need to buy your passage north. If Kaila sees that you have it in safe keeping, you may not lose her."

How could Gunni hold him like this still? Choked with disappointment, he pocketed the coins. He mumbled something about practicing tricks with the bear. He could not spend all the day reassuring a girl who wore her feelings like a hedgehog's bristles.

But when he returned to Tailor's Close and found that Dodder had decided to put off the matter of the bear's teeth so that the rest of their preparations could go forward smoothly, Wat gave no more thought to Kaila. She would be easier now that she need not worry over the bear.

He took up the ball and began to play with the bear again. Little Robin begged to be allowed to join in, but Wat didn't dare to let him too near. If the bear was annoyed or startled, she might swing her paw with stunning force. To distract Little Robin, Wat showed him the dragon tooth. The child was enthralled. "Look!"

he shouted to Nettle. "Look!" he bade Kaila as she came toward them.

Kaila peered at Wat's treasure, then touched it with one finger. "It is a bear's tooth," she said.

"Nay," Robin informed her. "It is a dragon's tooth." He turned to Wat for confirmation.

"That is so," said Wat. "A dragon's tooth. It cures many ills."

Kaila cast him a look of utter scorn. "It is the dog tooth of a bear." Her face closed.

Wat could tell she was thinking of the cub's teeth all over again. She would set herself against him now, and there was nothing he could do about it. Then let it be, he thought, weary of her, tired of the burden. Surely he was free now. He had given the Mirth Mongers the Writ and Gunni her bride price. Those gifts were riddings.

He turned back to the bear and sent her scrambling after the ball. They played until it was time for the final show for the fair.

This time Dodder led the performance on the green. Men and boys were still playing at stilts when he ran onto the grass in his rags and tags and donkey ears. Dogs darting in and around the stilters upset the last of them, until finally Dodder alone claimed the open space. Merchants and peddlers shouted hoarsely to draw the crowds and their open purses. The solitary minstrel sang lustily until his song was drowned out by a squealing pig under the knife. Through all of the frenzy of this final fair day, Dodder cartwheeled and flip-flapped with such vitality that his body took on the look of a fish with its tail in its mouth.

Dodder was still in motion when he signaled Wat to begin the game of ball with the bear. Crying, "Fish!" each time the bear caught the ball, Wat gradually moved toward Dodder, who quit his tumbling to act the fool. He chased first one way and then another. The crowd cheered whenever he fell flat on his face, and it cheered each time Wat outwitted him. Suddenly Dodder threw himself to the ground and pummeled the grass with his fists. Calling the bear, Wat walked right over the prostrate fool. The crowd gasped as the bear followed in his footsteps. She stepped across Dodder as she might have clambered over a stone. Yet she never touched him. Then Wat dropped the ball. Slowly Dodder raised his head and crept toward it. Glancing nervously at the bear, Dodder snatched the ball up and ran from the green.

Now it was up to Wat to keep the crowd's attention while Dodder changed his costume and all the other Mirth Mongers made ready for their final performance. He went through the feats of the previous days, taking his time and enjoying the fun of them. He seemed to be two people, one there on the grass with the bear, the other somewhere in the crowd where he had stood in past fairs craning for a good look at the games and mummery. The watching boy was thrilled to know the one with the bear. But the boy on the green was too intent on his work to admit the inner excitement. He calculated every move. Taking chances, he played the bear beyond the limits of their practice, and she responded.

He knew that she might sulk when the end came. She could even swat him enough of a dig to let him know she was annoyed. So he watched her closely. Finishing the performance with the bear on her back, her forepaws clutching her hindpaws, he slithered onto her belly and arranged himself the same way. When the bear rocked, Wat rocked, too, inside the curve of her body. Through the applause he heard the pipes and tabor. He tried easing the bear down, but she was wound too tight now and would not hear him. In the end he had to fall from her and then scramble for his footing out of her reach. His heart was pounding, his face running sweat. But they were done. They were fine. And now he was able to coax the bear to come away.

Befogged and breathless, he turned to watch the Mirth Mongers begin their dance. Beside him, Kaila murmured to the bear. He knew they were supposed to leave at once and make the bear ready for the journey. While everyone gathered for the harvest dance, he and Kaila were to take the bear to the gate and wait in the shadows for the Mirth Mongers. But Spurge and Toadflax were performing their most exciting stunts. The coins flew like hailstones; Little Robin and Bedstraw gathered them up. Wat told Kaila he wanted to watch the straw man show. After that, he would join her.

Wat knew that Kaila was glad to get away from the crowd, which parted to make way for the bear. The straw man came through the same opening. Tottering and whirling, he spilled ale from his cup and doused those who tried to give him a whack along the way. The bear was forgotten. All eyes were on him and on the Mirth Mongers. They tumbled over one another, vaulted and sprang, staggered and groped in mock blindness. For a while he led them a merry chase. And then they surrounded him.

Tap, tap, tap. The tabor announced the dance of the flails. There was no sound at all but that tap and jingle. The Mirth Mongers raised their flails and advanced on the straw man, on Furze. Dodder swung the flail like a whip, Dodder in his cloth of murrey and masked to be the Lord of Urris. The crowd exclaimed. Hands pointed. It was the first time in memory that this dance had been altered in any important way.

The dancers closed the circle. Spurge chanted about the man decked in straw. The crowd sighed. It was the old song, as old as the oldest stories. The flails became swords raised in the First Battle, each striking the next, yet never touching. The tapping quickened. The dancers backed away. They swung the flails like hooks swiping at the standing oats. At each swipe the straw man bent lower. Cut down by the reapers, he fell and fell until he lay in their midst.

"We cut down our father like the evening sun," chanted Spurge. These were the old words. The dancers converged so tightly, they had to flail in turn, thrashing in measured beat.

Like everyone else, Wat knew what to expect. The flails that had been swords and hooks would become swords yet again. The swords would form a roof over the straw man, while the dancers circled as the sun circles in its course across the sky. "We cut down our father like the evening sun." In a moment the dancers would leap back to reveal the straw man slipping his husk and rising up, all in green, like next year's shoots reborn in the earth.

The swords were locked together now. The flails were joined. Wat held his breath. In silence the dancers stepped and stepped. Then, with a clatter, they whirled apart. There lay the straw man, green at his shoulders.

Toadflax stamped his foot. It was the signal for the straw man to leap to his feet all green. Instead the dancer in murrey broke from the outer circle and stalked the straw man. Toadflax stamped once more. The straw man, his head still thatched, pushed the straw to his waist. The thrasher in murrey cloth flailed and flailed. Finally, under the rain of blows, the straw man grasped his bowed head and pulled off the thatch. Beneath it he wore a crown.

Shocked and stirred, people whispered among themselves. They could all see that the Lord was cutting down the King like the evening sun. He was there on his knees, half dead straw and half living green, clutching the crown to his head.

Spurge's voice rose above the whispers and murmurs. "Darkness comes. Winter comes. Who will set the green man free?"

With a roar the crowd surged forward. Wat was caught in the press of people. He felt someone grab his shoulder, but he could not turn. Someone shouted in his ear. "Go," he heard. "You have to make ready. Go!" The hand that gripped his shoulder was pulling him back and out of the human storm. Suddenly he stumbled, but he was clear of the mob now. Whipping around, he saw that it was Spurge who had pulled him clear. Now Spurge himself was engulfed.

Wat had to make his way into the marketplace before he could turn down to Tailor's Close. He passed the solitary minstrel, whose eyes were set on the odd stone, where the Steward and Clydog the Constable were talking together. So the minstrel was one of them after all, thought Wat. Dodder had been right to distrust him. The minstrel's face was chilling in its stony detachment. Never had he looked more solitary than now, at the edge of the writhing mob, intent on the Lord's servitors.

Wat ran all the way to Tailor's Close. Inside the yard he stumbled over something left near the gate. Groping ahead of him, he moved more carefully until he reached the mud wall of the cow shed. He called Kaila. There was no answer, no sound. He could smell bear all around him, but he knew the bear was not there.

He heard the Mirth Mongers on the run. Teasel came first, shouting to Bedstraw and Little Robin. Wat heard himself calling out, asking if Dodder was all right. Nettle spoke from the darkness. "Dodder is safe, but if the Lord himself were here now, they would thrash him to the ground."

Wat told them that Kaila and the bear were not here. One of them replied that she was probably waiting at the gate. She could not be far.

Wat nodded in the darkness. The gate. She had gone on ahead because he had failed to join her. Lurching toward the lane, Wat promised to find her and bring her to the gate if she was not there already. He stumbled again. Feeling the thing that caught him up, he touched an edge of fur and recognized his carrysack. Hoisting it on his back, he knew with dreadful certainty that Kaila had left it for him. The fur belonged to the leggings she had finished that afternoon. She did not expect to see him again.

He raced down to the bake house, which was empty. But Gunni had left a rushlight burning. That meant she would return soon.

When she came running through the door, her hair blown loose, her feet muddy to the ankles, she told him Kaila and the bear had gone.

"Gone where? We are supposed to have the bear at the gate."

Gunni drew a deep breath and let it out slowly. "The wrong gate, Kaila said. Her heart sends her north."

"But how could she?"

"I helped her," Gunni said. "Behind the salt house there is an apple tree beside the wall and a rope for those who must escape. Only a few of us know of it. I made a circle of the rope and Kaila attached it to the bear. The bear climbed high enough to drop from the tree to the ground on the other side of the wall. Then Kaila pulled herself up on the rope. When she went over, she landed on the bear. It broke her fall. I had told her that when she unfastened the rope from the bear to loop it under the root that stands broken on the other side.

"Then it will be found there. She will be caught."

Gunni shook her head. "In a while I will unknot the rope on this side and pull one end until it all comes back. Until I do, you see, there is a way north for you as well."

"For me?" he cried. "Why would I take that way?"

"Because you are free to choose. Like her."

Gunni was mocking him. She had ruined his chances with the Mirth Mongers. They would never want him now that the bear was gone. What choice did he have? "You could have stopped her," he charged.

"I told you. It was her choice. She is free." Then she added, "It is not the kind of freedom you can buy with a bride price. She does not live by our rules."

Torn and frantic, he said, "The Mirth Mongers are waiting at the gate."

"And they will have you, bear or no. You have a way with those games. Everyone speaks of it. Only you must choose."

He could feel her binding him to rules he would deny. With a choked cry he broke away and dashed out to the lane. He could hear the Mirth Mongers ahead of him, their voices subdued but urgent.

He told them what he had to, in cutting words. He could taste the bitterness of them.

Silence met his announcement. Then Dodder stepped out of the darkness. Wat saw that his head was wrapped in a cloth. When he drew closer, Wat saw blood on the cloth.

Dodder spoke in an undertone. "You will go with them?"

Wat could not answer.

Dodder told him gently, "Without you they will not go far. You know that."

Wat dug his fingers into his palms.

Dodder prodded him with something. It was the royal Writ. "Take it," said Dodder. "Even if you have no need of it now, you may later."

Wat felt tears on his face. "It belongs to the Mirth Mongers," he whispered.

"Then it belongs to all of us. Whatever road you travel, you are no less one." He touched the wetness on Wat's cheek and, with his thumb, erased the tears.

There was nothing more to be said. Already the din from the green and the marketplace was spreading through the town. Wat turned and pounded back to the bake house. Behind him he heard the south gate grating on the packed road. He clasped his hands to his ears to block the sound of the Mirth Mongers leaving.

Before he reached Gunni's doorway, she stepped out to meet him, a loaf under her arm. Side by side, wordless, they ran toward the garden with the apple tree, toward the rope and the wall.

PART IV

TRAVELER'S JOY

15

The rain that had held off all day began abruptly. It fell as though weighted, straight down. They stopped only long enough to put on their hooded jackets. Kaila behaved as if she didn't care whether Wat came with her or not. She just stumped along after the bear, who roved from side to side snatching up twigs and grass like a cow let out on the waste. Once in a while Kaila spoke a bear word. Sometimes the bear responded by climbing back onto the road and waiting, but more often she acted as if she hadn't heard.

"You should make her obey," Wat commented irritably.

Kaila may have shrugged her shoulders, but the hooded jacket only hinted at the gesture.

Spurred by her indifference, he snapped, "I did not give up the Mirth Mongers to lose the bear in the wilds."

Kaila didn't even turn her head to him.

The rain extended the darkness past daybreak. Wat could feel the penetrating chill on his face and legs, but he was otherwise warm and dry. It was the first time in his life that such a rain had not soaked him through.

The road rose gradually. Wat halted to gaze back toward Odstone. He saw nothing but a sheet of cold gray rain. On they trudged.

After a while Kaila shifted the weight of her pack and surged ahead to keep up with the bear. Determined not to run after her again the way he had after dropping over the wall, Wat timed his breathing to match his stride. He watched his knees rise more sharply as the way grew steeper. He even stopped once more to look back. He thought he saw something move, but as he stared, the figure lost its shape and dissolved in the downpour. Slogging on, he wondered how many more miserable days like this lay ahead of them.

In time it occurred to him that instead of looking behind, he should be keeping an eye on the glowering peaks above them. It was said that the mountain raiders who descended on travelers joined forces in the ambush. Afterward they fought over the spoils. Maybe the raiders would not think a boy and girl worth their trouble. Except for the bear, Wat realized, his heart sinking. They would know the bear was worth a king's ransom.

Ahead, where the road leveled off, Kaila had stopped. She seemed to be scanning the land that sloped down to the west. Following the direction of her gaze, he caught sight of a white blur. The bear had roamed far from their way.

"Call her," he ordered as he ran up to Kaila. "It is dangerous off the road. There could be raiders or hunters behind those rocks."

Cupping her hands to her mouth, Kaila gave a muffled shout. Then she shrugged off her pack and slithered down after the bear.

They came back slowly, the bear reluctant and distracted.

"What is wrong with her?" Wat demanded.

Kaila said, "She was digging roots. She is glad to be out of the cow shed, out of the town."

"Well, make her stay beside you."

"I cannot," said Kaila.

"Of course you can. You always have."

"It was too much," Kaila told him. "Too much people, too much games."

"It cannot have been too much. She loved to play those games."

Kaila shook her head. "She would have stopped. She is stopping now."

Wat had to prove Kaila wrong. He pulled a loaf of bread from

Kaila's pack and tossed it to the cub. One paw came out and grabbed it. "Fish," he commanded. The bear bent her head and bit off the end of the loaf. "Fish!" he shouted, sticking his face toward the bear and feeling the rain stream inside his hood. The bear swiveled on her hindquarters. He ran around to face her. "Fish, fish, fish!" he screamed. The bear took the bread in both paws and shoved it into her mouth.

"That's ours!" he cried, lunging at her and grabbing a handful of sodden bread. One paw slammed against his head. The hood cushioned the blow, but he was sent flying off the road. It was hard to get back on his feet. His neck was wrenched; his side and arm throbbed.

Kaila waited for him beside her pack. Climbing up to her, shivering, he realized his jacket was plastered with mud.

"Get that bread away from her," he stammered between chattering teeth.

"I cannot."

"It's for us."

"You should not have given it, then."

Seething, he scraped some of the mud from his jacket. He could feel the pouch beneath it, the sheathed knife. At that moment he wanted nothing more than to pull it out and drive the blade into the furry white breast. He watched the bear finish off the loaf. He watched Kaila hoist her pack. "Just keep her with us," he warned, his jaws aching as he clenched them to stop the chattering.

For a while the bear followed them, almost doglike and docile. Then she began to lag. Kaila had to speak to her again and again.

"Is she tired?" Wat finally asked.

"She is getting ready for the winter sleep."

"Not yet," Wat retorted. "No winter sleep along this way."

Kaila shot him a look he could not fathom. She pointed to the sky. "Can you give orders to the rain cloud?"

He did not bother to answer.

Over the following days the impression that someone was behind them on the road stalked at Wat's heels. Even after the rain lightened to a drizzle, the overhanging gray distorted everything in sight. He seldom even glanced back now. It was just a feeling, that was all.

Wat could smell the rot that crept into the skins he drew over himself at night. He envied Kaila, who burrowed under her cover like the bear folding herself into the nest she dug each night.

And then one morning he awoke from his fitful sleep to a pale, watery sunlight. Kaila was spreading their things on rocks and bushes. He knew they should be on their way without delay, but he couldn't bring himself to stop her. He gazed up past the sweep of barrens to mountains creased with silvered veins of water. Kaila pointed to ravens overhead. They converged at a spot not far from the road.

"Something killed," she told Wat. "Meat for us."

The bear followed her, but Wat remained beside the road, soaking up the feeble sun. He glanced back over the road but could not see beyond the long curve.

When Kaila called him, he saw no harm in clambering up after her. The sodden grass was slippery. Bracing his foot against a tough-stemmed willow herb, he twisted for balance. Something caught his eye in the distance. He found that he was high enough to see beyond the curve in the road. Far below and behind him, it slipped through the foothills like a long, wet eel. Something else. He stared hard. For a moment it seemed as if the eel were wriggling, impaled on a hook, but of course it was the other way around. The road was stationary. The hook moved along it. It walked.

"But it's just one person," he said aloud. That meant they had nothing to fear. He heard Kaila scolding the bear. He turned again to climb up to her, then stopped once more for another look. The hook, the walker, was no longer visible. He wanted to believe that he had imagined it, that the road was empty. He continued on until he saw what Kaila was standing over and cutting—the carcass of a deer. Away from her the bear crouched with a haunch from the animal.

"Look!" Kaila held up a slab of deer meat. Its stench kept Wat from coming closer. He told her he had seen someone on the road. They would have to keep moving.

She worked away with her knife, stopping from time to time to shove a bit of meat into her mouth. Then she held up something else. "Look!" she called again.

Halfheartedly he gazed up. A stick. Just a stick. He started to turn away, then whipped around again. "Let me see that," he called huskily. She waved the stick. Not a stick. An arrow.

He could hear the blood pounding in his head. How could she be so unwary? Someone had shot the deer. And recently, or the ravens and foxes would have consumed it. He opened his mouth to shout her back to the road, but the bear would never come now that she was sitting back and tearing meat from a bone. He could do nothing but wait.

Of course, after she had eaten her fill, the bear wanted to sleep. Wat was in despair over her, but Kaila sensibly set off along the road. Wat kept glancing anxiously all about him, but Kaila, who had eaten heavily, too, just kept plodding on.

Wat heard the bear before he saw her. She was squealing like a baby pig. She must have fallen asleep when they left her. Now she came scrambling so fast, her feet seemed scarcely to touch the ground. Reaching Wat first, still whimpering, she rose up and set her paws on his shoulders. Despite the bloodstained fur and the foul-smelling snout, he couldn't resist the appeal. He hugged her back. Next she galloped over to Kaila, who suffered a similar greeting. Then they continued on together.

At dusk the wind dropped. It was very cold. Shivering, Wat climbed into the fur leggings. He scanned the road. It seemed to be empty. Was that a trick of the half-light? A nighthawk soared low over the open scree, clearly visible. So he looked down the road once more. This time he saw the person following them. He seemed closer now. And there was something about him, even in the gathering darkness, something that Wat almost recognized. Frowning, he looked for a boulder or ledge they could spend the night behind. He told Kaila to leave the pack on the bear. He had to settle for a shallow depression in the ground. It was poor concealment, but when they huddled together, he thought they might blend in with the pitted terrain.

They woke under a light snowfall. Wat, instantly alert, saw no footprints. His stomach was so empty that it hurt, so Kaila produced a pouch containing the mixture she had pounded in the forest, berries and nuts and dried, pulverized meat. He dug out a fistful, devoured it, and reached for more. But she pulled the food away and told him to wait, that in a while it would seem like more. Wat had to admit that she was right, but he took another little bit of it. Against the lean times, he declared.

All that day the snow fell. It was fluffy and full of light and not unpleasantly cold. They stopped only once to rest, but Wat could not stretch out until he had hauled himself onto a huge outcrop so that he could look back over the road. The walker was clearly visible against the snow. And now Wat saw that it was the solitary minstrel.

Wat hurried back to tell Kaila.

"He may have food," she said.

He felt like shaking her. "Dodder thinks he is the Lord's spy."

"What is spy?"

"Someone who goes around listening and watching and then reports what he has observed."

"The Lord did not need a spy," Kaila said. "There were many to observe and report. What have we to fear from him here?"

Wat couldn't tell her, but he insisted that they move right on.

Late in the day the snow stopped falling. A fresh wind from the northeast swept the snow into drifts that dulled each bush and rock. When they finally stopped for the night, they found that the drifting snow had also blurred the edge of the landshelf below the road. As there was no level ground on the upland side of the road, they had to search for a place along the landshelf that was wide enough to keep them well away from its edge, for it overhung a deep gorge. The footing was treacherous, the view down the steep mountainside dizzying.

The snow and wind and height seemed to excite the bear. First she rolled, then she explored along the cliff edge until she found a second, narrower shelf that jutted out just below her. There she carved a nest for herself. Her digging raised and extended the edge of snow above her. Wat and Kaila noted the effect; they avoided that edge.

When the bear had finished packing the snow around her nest, she clambered back up to play. Charging at them, head down, she scooped snow ahead of her that plowed into them. Laughing, they drew her to the road, separated, and took turns commanding her to charge first one and then the other. After a while she collected more snow to shovel down to her nest. They avoided the path she made; it was hard and slippery. By the time she finished sliding and scooping the snow, all the bloodstains were washed away and her fur had the look of fresh milk with the creamy froth on top.

Once she had curled up inside her snowy den, Wat and Kaila, wrapped in all the skins Kaila had brought, settled themselves close to the road. As usual, Kaila dropped right off to sleep. But Wat's cold feet kept him awake for a while. He longed for morning.

He resisted opening his eyes, but Kaila seemed to want him awake. He groaned and flung off the hand that shook him. Only it came back. Its grip was brutal.

Then he knew the hand was not Kaila's. Instinctively he hunched over. He had a sudden, brief vision of the bear cub cowering in the corner of Stirk Close while her twin was clubbed to death. Yet there was no struggle here. He was simply yanked to his knees. He tried to shake off the hand that pulled him and held him down at the same time; but otherwise everything was strangely quiet. It was not fully light yet, the still gray time before sunrise.

"We will take the bear," said a man behind him.

Wat twisted around, only to be wrenched back on his knees.

"Just tell us where it is and how to bind it, and you can go along."

"Kaila," he said. "The girl."

"We have her. We take her and the bear."

"What have you done with her?"

"Let him up," said the voice.

Wat staggered to his feet. Five men. Five big men, one of them standing over Kaila, who was still on her knees. She was looking away from the bear's nest. Wat did the same. He said quietly, "If you hurt her, the bear will kill you. At best, the bear will do you little good unless you can make it perform."

The leader said to Wat, "It will fetch a mighty price, tricks or no."

Wat drew a long breath. He spoke like one instructing a dull-witted listener. "It can fetch a mighty price if you know its speech. Otherwise you have only a wild beast, and a dangerous one."

All the men laughed. One said, "We have fought wolves. Do you think we fear a single bear?"

"It has human reason," Wat informed him. "It is a warrior bear."

"It follows you like a dog."

"And so might it follow you if you learn its ways."

"Then we will take you as well, and you can teach us. What tricks will the bear play?"

"None, so long as you hold the girl. But if you let her go, I will show you one or two bear feats."

The leader ordered Kaila released.

"Now step back," Wat directed, his arms sweeping them toward the road. When none of them responded, he said, "You will be in the bear's way, and that will not be pleasant."

The men scuffed through the snow until they were spread along the road. Wat called the bear, who stretched and roared a yawn. Then she shook herself. It took some coaxing to get her to dance on her hind legs. When she began to move more freely, Wat had her crouch down so that he could leap over her. While he played with her, he watched the men. They leaned on their cudgels or dropped them and folded their arms. They muttered remarks that Wat could not hear.

Suddenly Wat fell in a pile of snow. The bear galloped over to him, faltered, and seemed to stumble. Instead of leaping, she straddled him. Wat heard the expected gasps from the men. As soon as the bear walked off, he called Kaila to his side. The bear vaulted over them with ease.

"I need more people," said Wat. "Two of you down with us."

"You must think us stupid," said the leader.

"Between us," said Wat. "We would be the first to be hurt."

The leader spoke to the others. Two men came and crouched down in the snow between Kaila and Wat. Again they commanded the bear, and she vaulted effortlessly.

"More," demanded Wat. "It is not yet enough."

"Not now," said the leader. "There is time for that later on."

"You fear the bear," said Wat considerately. "You sent two men, but you yourself fear the bear."

An argument broke out among the men. Then the leader swaggered over to the group with the bear. "Hurry, then," he said.

Wat nodded agreeably. "I will show you this time, and then you will give the command so that the bear will learn to obey you. He cried, "Leap the frog!" The bear backed off and vaulted once more. When she landed, she had to dig her claws in the packed snow to stop herself. Wat jumped up. "That was close," he said. "We must give the bear a running start. Here, like this." He gestured Kaila and the others onto the smooth path the bear had made. Glancing over at the two remaining men, a thought seemed to strike him. "Do you want to try, too? You can leap us first."

When they shook their heads, Wat said, "Of course. You might not be able to clear us all. The bear would show you up."

The leader said, "If you are planning some trick—"

"Of course I am planning a trick," Wat retorted. "You asked me to show you what this bear can do."

One of the remaining two declared, "I can jump as far as that bear." He came running, but his foot caught the head of one of his crouching companions and he tumbled onto the rest. There were shouts and grunts. The leader called the fellow a clumsy lout, and the one left standing burst out laughing. At that, all the others glared up at him.

It was more than Wat could have hoped for. He said mildly, "Maybe you should let the bear have the first turn and then see if you can do better." The four in the snow with him all agreed and insisted that the fifth join them. Wat checked them for raised shoulders or heads. He hauled Kaila out from between two men and placed her at the uphill end.

"What about you?" demanded the leader. "You think you can run off while all our heads are down?"

Wat said, "Where could I run to? I will put myself wherever you say."

"Where the bear will see you, since it would not hurt you."

Wat moved himself to the position nearest the oncoming bear. Kaila was next to him. He called to the leader to say the command.

"Leap the frog!" the leader barked.

Wat nudged Kaila, who uttered a single bear word as the cub rushed toward them. The bear slid to a halt.

"What happened?" demanded the leader, anger rising in his voice.

"You are strange to the bear," said Wat cheerfully. "You must sound very commanding, very strong."

The other men showed signs of restlessness, but by now the leader was determined to make the bear perform for him. Wat nudged Kaila again and mouthed the word: "Charge!" There was no time for an answering nod. The leader bellowed his command, while Kaila and Wat together cried their command to the onrushing bear and then rolled out of her path.

The bear bore down on the huddled men with such force that all five were caught and plowed in a wad of snow that went hurtling down the slide and over the edge of the landshelf. Kaila cried out as the bear dropped to the narrow ledge below, but she was able to claw herself to a stop. Standing sideways, she peered over the gorge where the men still tumbled and slid and fell. Then she looked up at Wat and Kaila, as if she weren't sure she had played her part to their liking.

"Well done!" Kaila shouted, without resorting to the bear speech.

Wat grinned at both of them. "Well done!" he echoed.

"Well done!" That was another echo, another voice.

Still on their hands and knees, Wat and Kaila froze. Wat thought only of more raiders.

"No time to spare gloating, though," the voice declared.

Not raiders, thought Wat. Turning, he faced the minstrel. In spite of his suspicions, relief flooded him. Even if the minstrel did serve the Lord of Urris, he was but one man here. Wat preferred to have him in sight rather than trailing them.

The minstrel began collecting the cudgels and bows and arrows. He twanged one of the bows, set it down, and tried another. He said, "We must bury what we cannot carry away with us. Some of those outlaws may come back to look for their weapons."

Wat said, "We should be on our way. When they return, they will be very angry."

The minstrel smiled. "I think it will not be soon."

They gathered up everything. The cudgels were too heavy to carry, and the bear looked as though she had finished pleasing them for a while. The only thing to do was to burn the wooden handles and staves and bury blades and stone heads. They scraped away enough snow to get a fire started. The minstrel, remarking that they should not waste the fire, chose a bow and some arrows, and clambered up the steep incline across the road. By the time he returned with one hare and two plump ground birds, there was a good bed of coals to cook them on.

While they ate, a tiny monkey head peeped out from the neck of the minstrel's tunic. The minstrel rummaged in his sack and pulled out a handful of oats. A long-fingered paw appeared. With delicate jabs the monkey picked one kernel at a time from the minstrel's palm.

Kaila, who had gorged the day before, only nibbled a bit of fowl. The minstrel and Wat ate hugely. Every bone was sucked clean before it was thrown to the bear.

"You are thoughtful, lad," the minstrel finally observed.

"Yes," answered Wat, but he couldn't say that he had been considering what a skilled archer this minstrel was to have fetched this game so quickly.

When the minstrel asked their names, Wat pointed to Kaila before she could speak and blurted, "Sea Kale." Then, with dignity, he said, "I am Traveler's Joy."

"And I am called Gadd Wistyn," responded the minstrel. "I have no Mirth Monger's name. My tricks are few. I have only the monkey for merrymaking. And I sing. You have a heard one of my ballads at the fair."

Wat nodded.

They sat a moment in silence, and then the minstrel spoke again.

"Since spotting you, I have wondered why you did not travel with your troupe."

Wat jumped to his feet. He told Kaila it was time to get the bear packed for their journey. In passing, he mentioned that he and the Mirth Mongers had parted for a purpose.

"A mighty purpose, I should think, to sever such fortunate ties."

Wat prodded the bear, who kept sinking down into the snow.

They had to tease and coax her to get her started. After that, she settled into a rolling gait that kept them scurrying to keep up. The minstrel brought up the rear of the little train. He had added a bow and arrows to his already sizable pack, yet he walked with a spring. Wat was more certain than ever that the man was not just a minstrel.

When they stopped to rest, the minstrel sang softly to the monkey, which sat grooming itself in the sun. At one moment Wat was wondering about the next ambush and warning himself that there couldn't be many raiders as doltish as those they had tricked this morning. At the next moment he was blinking groggily to keep from being lulled to sleep. As long as he could hear that song, he thought, he was still alert. But when he awoke, the singing had stopped. The minstrel was trying to call the monkey away from the bear.

The monkey paid no heed to Gadd Wistyn. The bear, lying on her back with her feet flopped sideways, seemed to ignore the tiny creature that poked here and there at one furry, black-clawed paw. Just as the long, restless fingers closed around a claw, Kaila swung down and plucked the monkey out of the bear's range. Wat could tell from the bear's distended toes and flattened ears that Kaila had been just in time.

On the road again, Wat warned the minstrel to keep the monkey out of the bear's reach. Gadd Wistyn nodded, but Wat doubted that he understood the danger. After all, he had seen Little Robin on the bear's back. He had seen all the games and antics on the green at Odstone.

Later, when the minstrel dropped behind, Kaila asked Wat why he didn't get the minstrel to tell him how much farther it was to the sea. Wat answered that the less the minstrel knew about their destination, the safer they would be.

"He has brought down game and shared it with you," she argued.

Wat gave up trying to explain.

At nightfall they were on a high plateau hemmed in by dark, snow-swirled crags. Both Wat and the minstrel eyed them uneasily. They agreed to take turns keeping watch. The minstrel accepted some of Kaila's skins and made a bed for himself in the open. Kaila slept near the bear. Wat leaned back against a rock and imagined figures marching around the peaks. But every time he stood up to peer more closely, he saw only shifting snow in the eerie moonshine.

"Will you take my bed now?" asked the minstrel as he stretched. "It is already warm."

Wat was glad for the ready bed, but he found it hard to be courteous. "Why did you follow us?" he asked in an undertone.

"I came after you," answered the minstrel. "It could not be avoided."

"Do you travel alone always?"

"Not always."

As they stood facing each other, Wat noticed for the first time a scar that contorted the side of the minstrel's face and drew the lid half over one eye. Before now he had assumed that the look was a kind of squint. But here in the bright-dark night, it reminded him of the falcon, Gyr. It was something he had sensed all along about this man. Gadd Wistyn had the sharp, calculating gaze of a bird of prey.

16

Each day brought changes in the terrain. The road was only a rough, narrow track, but the walking was easier now that it had begun its descent. As the jagged peaks receded, the highlands opened onto rolling hills. Hare and fowl abounded, and Gadd Wistyn shot whatever they needed to eat. He seemed less and less like a minstrel. Only the tiny monkey reminded Wat of his calling.

The monkey was not only flea-ridden, a condition Wat learned about the first night he used the minstrel's covers, but it stole anything it could lay its hands on. It was drawn to the bear, who clearly considered it a nuisance.

But the nights that wolves emerged out of the gloom and ringed the fire, Wat found himself glad to have the minstrel-archer along. Gadd Wistyn felt that the smell of the bear would make the wolves keep their distance. But when Wat sat up alone on his watch, he kept his eye on the shadow beasts loping in and out of the trees that crowded the roadside.

One frost-bound night, Wat and Kaila and Gadd Wistyn stayed longer than usual at their fire. There had been a fresh snowfall during the day. The snow was hard and stinging this time. Even with evergreens shielding them from the wind, all three travelers were chilled.

Wat wondered aloud what they would see if the trees were not there.

"The Vanishing Lake," said Gadd Wistyn. "You may yet see it glinting between the hills."

It was the first time that he had indicated that he knew this country.

Wat thought carefully before he spoke. "This road passes a vanishing lake?"

"Near it."

"That is where you leave us?"

"I will not leave you," Gadd Wistyn replied.

Wat drew a small breath and said evenly, "We are going to the sea."

The minstrel inclined his head. He did not dispute Wat's intent.

Wat said, "I will take the first watch."

Gadd Wistyn said, "I think we may all sleep through this night."

Wat tensed. Trying to sound offhand, he asked why they needed no watch.

"I have just said." The minstrel seemed a little testy. "We are close enough to the Vanishing Lake. There are watchers to keep any raiders away."

Watchers friendly to Gadd Wistyn? No doubt friendly to the Lord of Urris, too. There was only one thing to do, and that was to try to steal away with Kaila and the bear while Gadd Wistyn slept.

Wat threw off his coverlet. He would be too cold to sleep. He waited. He could hear sounds in the surrounding wood, but nothing like a human tread. Tonight even the wolves were silent.

Cramped with cold, he finally got up and shook Kaila awake, his finger to his lips. "Get the bear," he whispered. In an instant Kaila was up and moving. He shoved her things into her pack. They would not be able to load the bear.

Kaila's urgent whispers called him to her. "The monkey," she said. "It is with the bear."

The bear was drowsy and cross at being disturbed. Against her chest, wrapped inside the warm, thick forelegs, nestled the monkey.

"Distract the bear," Wat directed.

While Kaila scratched and rubbed and the bear grunted with pleasure, Wat dug deep inside the warm cavity. His fingers were so cold, he could hardly feel what was monkey and what bear. All was soft and dangerous. At last his stiff fingers closed on their quarry. Inserting the other hand, he tried to dislodge the monkey. He pried open the long fingers only to find that it gripped the bear's thick fur with its toes.

"Be ready," he warned Kaila. Then he hauled back as hard as he could. The monkey screeched; the bear reared up in fury. In the next moment the minstrel was standing over Wat shouting, "Get that bear!"

"Hush!" said Wat.

"Don't hush me!" rasped Gadd Wistyn. "That beast has my monkey."

Wat had the sense to say, "We know. We were trying to save it."

The bear was swaying and trying to pluck the nuisance from her fur.

Speaking bear words, Kaila approached slowly, her hands going out to the bear. It was a long stretch up to the chest and between the legs. Kaila spoke as she advanced. When she snatched up the monkey, it chittered a protest, while the bear uttered a low, throaty growl. Gadd Wistyn couldn't wait for Kaila to bring him the tiny creature. He lunged for it.

The bear reacted at once to the man swooping down on Kaila. The left forepaw shot out, caught the man's shoulder, and, with that single blow, toppled him. As soon as he was down, the bear was finished with him. She dropped onto all four feet to lick Kaila's face and hands.

Gadd Wistyn writhed in the snow. For a time Wat and Kaila could do nothing for him. When he finally quieted, they parted his torn garments. Claw marks raked his back and arm, oozing blood, but the worst injury seemed to be inside his shoulder. They made a litter out of bows and skins. Wat put the monkey in a food bag and pulled the strings tight. By sunrise they had the bear in a kind of harness and ready to haul her victim.

It was slow going. The bear was sulky now, and Gadd Wistyn, in dreadful pain, moaned horribly. Wat tried to ignore the moans and the monkey's muffled screams.

"I should have strangled the animal," he said to Kaila. "As soon as it started to howl."

But like the bloody claw marks, the monkey was a surface irritant. What really troubled Wat was that now they could not abandon Gadd Wistyn. It meant that they had to head for the Vanishing Lake where, Gadd Wistyn assured them between gritted teeth, help was to be had. Most of the time, though, he could not speak at all. He simply yelled whenever the litter struck a rock or tilted and bounced through a rut.

Eventually they stopped to give him a rest. Kaila tried to ease the shoulder with a snow bath, but it only soaked the rest of Gadd Wistyn's tunic and started him shivering. Yet his face glistened with sweat. Kaila shook her head. There were plants to stop bleeding and leaves to draw heat, but it was past their growing time. Suddenly Wat remembered his dragon's tooth. It might quell the agony.

Bending over the litter and its groaning burden, Wat held out the tooth and touched it to Gadd Wistyn's shoulder. The man gave a feeble cry.

Wat said, "This heals the falling sickness. Let me bind it to your shoulder. It may ease the pain and make it well."

Gadd Wistyn was too miserable to protest.

Wat tried not to hurt him more, but when he tore strips from the shredded tunic and wound them around the injured shoulder, the minstrel gave a terrific shout and fell back senseless. Wat worked rapidly, pulling cloths as tight as he could so that the dragon tooth would not slip out. Then he bound the bandaged shoulder to the litter pole.

Continuing on, the surface of the track improved; now the litter did not bounce quite so badly. But when the bear paused to sniff the air, each time she started up again with a lurch, the dragging litter was jarred. Just as well, thought Wat, that the minstrel knew nothing of it. But he asked Kaila to slow the bear so that the halts would not be so abrupt.

"She is too fond of the downhill," he remarked.

"It is not the downhill that speeds her," Kaila replied, though she couldn't say what it was that excited the bear.

The next time the bear drew up, she tried to rise as well. Wrenching herself as if to break free from the litter shafts, she threw off one bow. Now she could stand to her full height. She seemed intent on something ahead that they could not see. Her head held still, the long, sloping muzzle pointing toward the horizon.

"Get her down!" cried Wat as he scooted around to the dislodged bow. It was whipped out of his hands so fast, his fingers stung. In the next moment the bear was galloping down the road, and the man in the litter was hurled onto his wounded side with terrible force. He screamed. Wat hadn't even realized that he had regained his senses.

The bear and her lopsided cargo plummeted along the track, Wat and Kaila racing to catch up. Almost as suddenly as she had charged off, the bear wheeled and lashed out at the litter. But by then it had already dumped its passenger. Kaila flung her arms around the bear's neck. She hung on that way, prepared to be dragged. Wat knelt beside the injured man, touched him.

Gadd Wistyn opened his eyes. He stared at Wat a moment. "Is it finished?" he asked hoarsely.

Wat supposed he meant this punishing ride. He said, "Nearly."

Gadd Wistyn, his face no longer contorted with pain, only bleached and filthy and drenched, nodded weakly. His good hand reached across with gingerly caution and touched the shoulder. "Help me up," he whispered.

Wat feared that if he moved the man, he would drive him into darkness again. Yet Gadd Wistyn had touched his shoulder without so much as flinching.

"Did you hear me?" Some of Gadd Wistyn's usual imperious tone had returned. "I would sit up."

He gasped as Wat eased him upright, but then he tried to move his arm a little. He nodded again. "You are right," he said. "It is nearly cured."

Wat's jaw dropped. The shoulder moved. He could see that the claw marks were less distended now that the shoulder could rotate again.

"I suppose," said the man, "it may be tender for a while."

Wat shut his mouth. Not trusting himself to comment on this miracle, he unhitched the remaining shaft of the litter and left it beside the track. With Kaila's help he raised Gadd Wistyn to his feet. They walked with a good deal of the minstrel's weight on Wat. It was clumsy going along that way, for the injured arm was swollen and full of heat. Kaila was torn between keeping up with the bear, who surged ahead, or staying behind to offer a guiding hand.

"This shows," Wat muttered to her, "that it is a true dragon tooth."

She wiped the black hair from her eyes and shook her head, only to cover her eyes all over again. "Bear's," she hissed. "And the tongue of the bear would heal even more."

Gadd Wistyn, grunting with the effort to keep himself going, did not hear this exchange. As far as he could tell, his recovery was a simple marvel.

By the time they reached the place where he was to leave the track, the bear was so far ahead, they had lost sight of her. Wat tried to use this as an excuse for letting the minstrel carry on alone. But just then Gadd Wistyn stumbled, and it was apparent to all three of them that if he fell, he would never be able to regain his footing unaided. Wat had to let Kaila continue on after the bear while he helped Gadd Wistyn over the trackless ground through the trees.

Wat kept warning himself that the man who leaned on him was walking him into a trap. But he could only keep going. As he listened for Kaila and the bear, it occurred to Wat that those two might yet avoid the men Gadd Wistyn sought.

"Here," said Gadd Wistyn, ponting to a narrow path that edged a gentle slope. "We follow this across Bogshill until we come to Gosty Meadow and Deer's Leap."

Wat eased him onto the ridge. Gadd Wistyn frowned with concentration. Any twist or thrust squeezed the breath out of him. Bit by bit they skirted the hillside. There ahead lay open grassland, an outcropping of rock at its summit. Gadd Wistyn nodded. "Gosty Meadow," he said. "And Deer's Leap at the head of it." He had to climb sideways, inching his way through meadow grass still tinged green.

Wat could see why it was called Gosty Meadow, for all around them the grass shivered as though alive, and the surrounding hills cast shadows like moving wraiths. Far below them, pocketed between the grassy slopes, the lake spread its fingers through a bog. Wat could see the glint of water in among the tall reeds and sedges. Where did the water stop and the land begin? Wat couldn't tell. Except beneath the brow of Deer's Leap, where all was rock, everything was stirring and fluid.

While they were descending, Gadd Wistyn slipped and jarred his shoulder. The sweat broke out again. Wat let him down carefully on his good side. Gadd Wistyn closed his eyes in relief.

"Will someone come for you here?" Wat asked.

"Not yet," Gadd Wistyn answered. "Not while the lake is there."

Wat sat down beside him. There was still no sign of Kaila and the bear. Were they waiting, too? The sun was sinking, the shadows lengthening. He supposed it was only a matter of time before Gadd Wistyn's friends, Havel's henchmen, showed themselves. It seemed to Wat that while he had come all this great distance, he had not advanced one step. The only difference was that now he had more to lose. He sank back. For a while he propped his head on his hand. When his arm grew stiff, he dropped down beside Gadd Wistyn. He had not slept at all last night. Now, suddenly, sleep overtook him.

He awoke to voices. Beside him, Gadd Wistyn was just trying to rise. Wat leapt up to help, but Gadd Wistyn growled a surly rebuff. He spoke out to the voices. "Here," he called. "Rescue me from the kind assistance of this groggy lad."

The men who clambered up from the lake looked much like the raiders, except that these carried lances and swords. There were many of them, and they all seemed to walk right out of the lake.

The lake! Wat stared down in amazement. Where the water had spread itself like an open palm and shoved its shiny gray fingers into the reeds, Wat saw only a valley of mud. There seemed to be a kind of road through it made of paving stones. The stones glistened wetly in the failing light.

The men aiding Gadd Wistyn took their time with him, but Wat was hurried down a steep embankment and onto a log bridge half submerged in the mud. The logs were loosely lashed together. They tended to sink underfoot but were buoyed up at the same time by those which bore no weight. Wat slipped and slithered and threw out his arms for balance, but the men with him seemed used to the bobbing.

They led him on to the paving stones, which were solid as bedrock. Here they pushed him quickly along toward the rocky outcrop beneath Deer's Leap. Only when he came under its shadow did Wat see that the road continued on into the rock and that the rock itself was hollow.

The men strode into darkness softened here and there by torches set in stone sockets. Wat couldn't help thinking of Kaila and the bear. Even if Kaila set out to find him, she would never see this passage. Did that mean she was safe for now?

The tunnel turned and turned once more. Wat caught a glimpse of a second passage, but he could not peer into it, for his captors kept him moving. The way began to rise. Ahead, the dimness brightened. They walked out onto an expanse of trodden meadowland. There were horses and small pens with sheep and pigs. Wat was led past these toward a great earthen embankment with an entrance cut through it. On the other side of it Wat found himself looking up at yet another wall, this one like a mountain of stone rearing straight up and dwarfing them all.

The gateway through this fortress was tall enough for a horse and rider, but in that enormous reach of stone it seemed no larger than a rat hole. There were timbered gates with massive iron hinges and bolts. The gates stood open, but Wat shrank from entering. The only walls he had been inside were made of sticks and mud. Now he felt as small and helpless as a child thrust inside a potter's oven. Sweat soaked his back and legs. He dug his fingers into his palms. When the men dragged him through, he could almost feel the crushing weight of that stone.

He was led into a courtyard with a life of its own. He saw two smiths at a forge. He saw men and women stretching oxhides. There were huts of stone and shelters made of sticks and mud just like those in Odstone. He tried to fix his eye on them so that he could forget the huge wall that caught them all in its circle.

There was also one large hall made partly of stone and partly of palings. Its roof was thatched, but it was open at each end. He was taken around to the side of it and shoved into a shed. Light filtered through the chinks in the flimsy wall. He shared his prison with a pair of geese. One stretched a long neck out and hissed menacingly.

He listened to voices and the sounds of hammering. He picked up separate words but could make no sense of them. Somewhere close by, chickens squabbled. Comforting sounds. Slowly his fists unclenched. And as he rid himself of the clammy dread a sound more distant than the voices and the chickens and the hammering came surging through to him. He had never heard anything like it. It made him listen in a new way, until he could feel its curious rhythm and could sense the coming of each muted crash, with the long hissing afterward like a storm's last breath.

When the shed door was yanked open, it was already dark, the courtyard stabbed here and there by the flickering light of torches. He was led into the great hall and over to the fireplace, where he stood warming his hands and waiting for the men seated on a bench across from him to take some notice of him.

At length one looked up at him. "Gadd Wistyn," said this spokesman, "has told us a little about you. And your companions."

This was a statement, not a question. Wat simply looked at the speaker, who was dressed like all the others in rough woolen homespun.

The man gestured at Wat's leggings and hooded jacket. "I have not seen garments like those before. What land are they from?"

"Thyrne," answered Wat.

"Where in the Kingdom of Thyrne do folk dress like that?"

Wat said, "These garments were made by someone from the Land of the White Falcons."

The spokesman nodded. Wat kept his eyes on him, noting the reddish hair shot through with gray, the gray beard, and the deep eye sockets in a face as creased as old parchment.

The spokesman said, "We wonder why you come this way with the ice bear."

Wat didn't know where to begin or what to leave out, so he said nothing.

"Tell us," urged the spokesman, his tone almost civil, but with a hint of pressure in it. "Whose bear is it?"

"You know," Wat retorted, flashing with anger. "You know that Havel had it seized. You must know all that. The she-bear and her cubs were not the Lord's to condemn, not his."

"Whose, then?"

"Why, the King's."

"The King's. I see. And are you then in the service of the King?"

Wat could feel the heat rising in him. He stepped back from the fire. The spokesman stayed where he was, at his ease on the bench, his voice mild and civil.

"I am in no man's service," Wat answered shakily.

"You are not bound?"

"I am free," Wat pronounced in too small a voice.

This brought a smile to the worn face across from him. Wat realized at once how puny he must look, how absurd it was to claim freedom as he stood captive inside this fortress.

"Where do you come from?"

"I lived with the baker's widow in Odstone. Then the Mirth Mongers had me with them. I may join them again."

"Why are you not with them now?"

"They went south."

The gray brows drew together. "You answer me, but you tell me nothing. What are you called?"

"Traveler's Joy."

After a brief silence the spokesman repeated the name. "You did not bring much joy to your traveling companion."

Wat tensed. He did not know which companion was meant.

"Have you nothing to say?" demanded the spokesman, rising now. To Wat's dismay all the others rose as well. Something was going to happen.

"Your companion, Gadd Wistyn, did not enjoy the bear."

Relief that it was that companion, and not Kaila, loosed Wat's tongue. "Oh," he said, "yes, that. But it was the monkey, his own monkey."

The bushy eyebrows shot up. "The little monkey drew such deep red stripes in the flesh?"

"Yes. No. The monkey caused the trouble. Gadd Wistyn would not wait. The bear thought he was attacking the girl."

"Ah, the girl," said the spokesman. "Tell me how she comes to be with you."

"She is with the bear," Wat replied stiffly. "Her father was bear-keep. From the Land of the White Falcons."

The spokesman nodded. "So she must belong to the King as well."

"She belongs to no one. In her land the people have neither lords nor kings."

"She is in my land now," the spokesman pronounced.

Wat drew himself as tall as he could to dispute the man's claim. "If the Lord of Urris takes what he has no right to, does he truly possess it?"

The spokesman drew back in surprise. "Go on."

Thinking he had nothing to lose now, Wat said, "Kaila's father came of his own accord with gifts for the King of Thyrne. Those who brought him made him a slave. If the King knew this, he would understand that Kaila's father was wronged. The King was wronged. They all were."

The spokesman waved his companions aside. He drew closer to Wat. "If this is true," he remarked softly, "then the bear belongs to the King."

Wat could not dispute this. Nodding, he said, "In a way."

"Is there another way I am not acquainted with?" Indignation had crept into his tone, a trace of impatience as well. "You must know, lad," he went on more briskly, "that the King has pressing matters to deal with besides the disposition of one ice bear, which is his. Which is undeniably a gift to the crown. There is the larger matter of moment to do with the disposition of the Lord of Urris. Do you follow me, lad?" The voice rose. "Do you mark me?"

Wat was so baffled by the shift in tone that he heard the words in a scramble. He looked past the spokesman to the others, who were all regarding their leader now. Wat shook his head. "I do not understand." He hated the way he sounded like a little boy.

The spokesman turned a ring on his second finger, so that an oval mount showed for the first time. He thrust his hand out across the dying fire. "Does an ignorant lad like you know the import of this sign?"

Wat had to stand on tiptoe. He saw the marks he could not read. He saw the hand figure he had come to know so well on the Writ he carried. "The royal signet," he murmured. Did it mean that the King had fallen victim to the Lord's henchmen? "Has something befallen the King?" he asked in a whisper. "They await him."

The spokesman turned the signet back to his palm. "Gadd Wistyn brings us word of that readiness. We know that Havel has crossed the kingdom with lands he has seized and lords he has joined to his plot. He looks to the south for our coming. We will sweep down from the north. From here. And, yes, it will be soon, now that the people are aroused."

Stunned, Wat gazed up at the speaker. "But," he stammered, "but I thought . . . You did not seem . . ." His voice dropped to a hush. "I did not think to see the King. Ever."

The King of Thyrne nearly smiled. "So you had not rehearsed the encounter? It is customary to bend the knee at such meeting."

But Wat was too stupefied to obey. He just stood rooted, amazed.

17

Wat had scarcely heard the King declare, "You will stay within the wall just now," though the note of warning was clear. Wat found ready food and ready conversation among those who went about their tasks by torchlight. He squatted beside first one and then another, gathering scraps of information. He learned that when the King sailed homeward from his long wars across the seas, he had swung his vessels to the west and then set a course toward the northernmost reaches of his kingdom. He had put his horses out on an island and moved into this stone fort, which had been built long, long ago by another king to defend the land from sea raiders.

Wat's head was full of disjointed thoughts and impressions. If the King had sailed past the southern tip of Thyrne and on into the western sea until in time he could head northeast, that must mean that if you went far enough, you would find that all the seas were connected. Would that be true of the Frozen Sea as well? Maybe if he and Kaila and the bear had gone with the Mirth Mongers, they would really have found a way north. Wat doubted that Kaila's heart, which had sent her so firmly and obstinately on a direct course northward, could rescue her now.

Wat staggered back to the goose shed and dropped onto the straw. It seemed as though he had just begun to sleep when someone shook him awake. Rubbing his eyes, he blinked at the chinks of light through the wall and wondered where he was. It was his first sleep under a roof in so long that the inside dimness was confusing.

He was sent into the great hall again. The King, along with others, was poring over a map spread out on the floor. Looking up at Wat's approach, the King nodded curtly and said, "You must bring the bear and the girl."

"I do not know where they are."

The King gestured at one of his men, who jumped up and led Wat out the far end of the hall. Ahead of them the great encircling wall stood tall and dark, but Wat could hear beyond it the strange, ponderous surge that had filled the goose shed with its sound. The man leading Wat mounted steps that hugged the inside of the wall and led to a platform where two men garbed in heavy mantles stood watch. The wind was so sharp, it brought tears to Wat's eyes. The man who led him put out a steadying hand and, with the other, pointed past the platform.

Wat edged closer, pushing against the wind. And there, beaten to a froth, lay the blackest water he had ever seen. He shivered with excitement. He saw a few islands in the middle distance, each ringed with white. He saw the black water graying on the horizon, stretching away to the pale, limitless sky. The waves surging and crashing were like a monstrous pulse.

"Look," said the man. "The bear and the girl. You must fetch them."

Wat drew his gaze from the heaving water to see where the man pointed. Far below, past the rocks that jutted out from the base of the wall, he saw Kaila and the bear on a patch of sand between two sea-splashed boulders. The bear, sitting with her hind legs splayed forward, was draping herself with some kind of ropy weed that lay all about her. She seemed to be eating it, too. Kaila stood back from the water that swirled around the bear in great wheels of foam.

Wat cupped his hands to his mouth, but the man said, "She will not hear you. The waves make such a racket."

Wat watched the bear scooping up another weed from the shallows. It seemed to slip from her grasp and slide seaward, but she pounced to retrieve it as though it were living prey. Then she rolled with it and splashed in a frenzy of joy. And it came to Wat that she must feel that she had come home. He said, "I cannot bring her. I will not."

The man led Wat back down the stone steps and into the hall. Wat felt dazed, as if part of him were still out there in the wind. The waves were in his ears now. His head was full of the sea and the bear's joy. He saw the King on his knees with his men marking the map. This time the King did not even glance up. Wat was sent from the hall.

Walking around the courtyard, he began to ask questions again. When would the King ride south to crush the Lord of Urris? One worker after another shrugged. Only the King and his advisers knew. But more shiploads of footmen would arrive before he marched southward. What else was the King waiting for? Wat demanded.

"You have many questions," said a voice from behind him.

Wheeling, Wat faced Gadd Wistyn. He was clean and freshly garbed, the injured arm bound to his chest.

"Ask me what you seek to know," Gadd Wistyn went on, "and leave these men to their tasks."

Wat cast aside all caution. "Why did you not say you served the King?"

"I was sworn to conceal my errand when I took the garb of minstrel to gather information for the King. He had known for some time that the Lord of Urris was overreaching his power."

"Then why did not the King put an end to Havel's misrule before now?"

"From the south? Havel would have been warned far in advance. Much of Thyrne would have been under the sword, forests and farmland destroyed."

"But people are being destroyed all the while," Wat cried.

"That was necessary, too. If the King's armies come down from the mountains like raiders, they will only succeed if the people of Urris are angered enough to rise up against the Lord. They had to feel the full weight of him leaning upon their lives before they were ready, as they now seem to be in Odstone. That discontent will serve the King."

Wat hated the way Gadd Wistyn spoke. He sounded so indifferent to the suffering of the people. He seemed to care only for its effect, for the discontent that would serve the King. Wat said, "The King would not have waited like this if he had known how ill-used the people are and how they look for his coming." Wat thought of Ulf and Gunni. He said, "They believe the King will put an end to Havel's tyranny."

Gadd Wistyn tilted his head. "That belief is useful as well."

"So the King," mumbled Wat, so choked he could barely speak, "is like other men, after all."

"Good," said Gadd Wistyn. "You are slow to learn, but that is a start."

"If he does not care what happens to the folk in Odstone, what makes him better than Havel, Lord of Urris?"

"An impudent question, but a fair one. The King cares for his land and his people and all their possessions, which are his. But he cannot count lives one at a time. Do you think that he who has fought beside beloved companions could stop to mourn each one that fell? If so, they would have fought in vain, for the battle would be lost. The King regrets the suffering and hardship in his kingdom. He seeks to put an end to it. But he must set his mind to the grander scheme, or fail his kingdom."

What would Gunni say to this? Wat wondered. At least she did not love the King the way the birdman did. The birdman was heartbroken, certain he had grieved the King. Was it possible that the King did not care?

"Now then," Gadd Wistyn finished, "attend to the bear. Do not try the King's patience. He would like to be generous with you for bringing the bear and helping me to safety. But understand that to him you are like an ant. If you dally, he may put his foot down. He may step on you."

Wat bowed his head to free himself from the predatory gaze. He said, "I must speak with him again. With the King." He did not then know what he would say about the birdman. He only hoped that it would serve Kaila and the bear at the same time.

Gadd Wistyn reminded Wat with chilling scorn that the King was not given to converse with bear-keeps or even with Mirth Mongers.

Wat forced himself to return Gadd Wistyn's gaze. "It is on another matter. It is a message. If he doubts me, ask him how he thinks I could have recognized his signet. He will believe then that I carry a message."

Gadd Wistyn turned so sharply that the little monkey on his shoulder had to fling its thin arms around his neck. Watching him stride into the hall, Wat wondered if the man's heart quickened for any living thing besides that dangling monkey. Oh, he served the King, of course, but not as the birdman must have, not for love. The thought came to Wat then that there was a time when he might have grown to be such a man. Before Gunni.

"You are free," Gunni had told him. How that had grated with him afterward. He had felt tricked. "You are free," she had informed him, charging him in the same breath with finishing what he had begun. "You are free," she had insisted, while she showed him the snare he had freely cast himself into. She didn't even have to tighten the cord. She let Kaila and the bear do that.

"Traveler's Joy!" Wat was summoned with a name that nearly swept right past him. But just in time it came around him like an arm catching him in its grip. Traveler's Joy! Yes!

The King did not wait for Wat to reach him before hurriedly declaring that he had little time to spend on this matter and that if Wat refused to fetch the bear, it would be killed. At least there would be the magnificent fur pelt. "But you should know, lad," the King continued, "that I have learned more of your doings. I know what risks you took to play the fool with the bear and the dangers you braved to bring the beast to me. You could have fled, or tried to, but you chose to remain with my injured messenger. For all of this I am prepared to offer you a good living. I fancy a performing ice bear. Though I have no court, nor time for entertainments now, the time will come when the bear could be a marvelous ornament at feasts."

Wat said, "But it was on another matter I sought your hearing."

The King waved impatiently. "Speak, then."

"It is about your Falconer."

"I have several falconers," the King replied stiffly.

"From long ago. With the white falcon, Gyr."

"Gyrfalcon!" Surprise and pain showed in the King's eyes. "I will not hear of the man. He betrayed me."

Wat saw the little birdman seated on an oak bough, his spindly legs dangling like white stems. The words spilled out, past history jumbled with the summer's events in the Forest of Lythe, everything Wat could recall.

The King paced back and forth, head down, his hand clasped to his face. Finally he threw himself on the bench and dropped his head in his hands. "All this time," he murmured. "Parted from so old a friend is loss enough. But to have believed he turned against me, that is more bitter than the loss itself." He looked up at Wat. "Suppose this man tricked you. Have you some sign or thing of his?"

Wat thought a moment. "Sire," he said finally, "I cannot read. It was the birdman who told me what your seal meant. It was he who read the words on the parchment. How else could I have known them? I would have had the Falconer himself to show you if he had not refused to come away, for he said you would have more need of him in the Forest of Lythe than in the royal mews."

The King stood up. "I will send someone for him." He paused, his eyes hard and distant. "Or maybe not for the present. Maybe he will serve me through this winter more fully than he realizes."

"Sire, he is not strong."

"Not strong? He has survived every misfortune."

Wat tried again. "Strong in heart, yes. But he is . . ." Wat's voice dropped. "He is like a bird, truly. His bones are thin."

"Well, it cannot be decided this moment—" The King broke off. He seemed to be hearing Wat's words as though for the first time. "We flew hawks together when we were young," he added in a whisper.

Wat said nothing. He knew the King was speaking to himself now. Wat waited.

Finally the King brought his attention back to Wat. He said, "Before now, there was much I would give you, a place in my court as bear-keep and mirth man. Surely you could not have hoped for more when you saved the bear from the gallows."

Wat could not bring himself to answer. To be the King's mirth man, to be protected and extolled, to do what he loved most—these were beyond anything he could have invented for himself at the time.

"Do I overwhelm you, then?" The King smiled. "It is fitting. For you have overwhelmed me. And if I could, I would match the gift you have given me."

Wat tried with all his might to summon the right, convincing words. "Sire," he began, "when I saved the bear from the gallows, I knew nothing. I thought the bear-keep's daughter an idiot girl. But without her there would have been no play of the Feast of Fools. Not with this bear. The tricks are mine, the wisdom is hers. She knows the speech of bears. She is especially wise in bear things." He faltered.

The King asked if Wat was requesting the girl as assistant bear-keep. Already his fingers were strumming on the sleeve of his homespun tunic. He had more than Wat and Kaila on his mind. Soon the royal attention would be directed elsewhere. Time was running out.

"Speak now," the King prompted. "Will you fetch the bear and the girl from the shore before the villagers grow sour against me? The bear has already shredded some fishing nets."

Stalling, Wat said, "The bear is not to be trusted among people.

If you confine her to small quarters, she will grow surly and then she will never perform."

"I know the ice bear is not to be trifled with," the King replied. "But if it does not serve me, its skin will line my mantle. I had the bears sent to the Forest of Lythe for their good as well as others. I do not favor a cowed beast. I would have my bear as proud as a warrior. And, I trust, as joyful as a traveler."

Wat said, "They think they are going home."

"For now this is their home."

"To the land of Kaila's people," Wat explained.

"Impossible," declared the King of Thyrne. "Are you asking me to let the bear go? That would leave me without my prize and you with my wrath. And do you know what would likely happen to the bear? It would be killed or captured and promptly sent to whatever court paid the highest price for it. Let the girl train you to the bear speech, and she can do what she likes after that. I will set you on one of the Islands of Tor for the rest of the winter, you and the bear and the girl. If the girl teaches you all she knows, she may go freely to the Frozen Sea."

Wat was dumbfounded. Could he learn Kaila's language and her lore? Those words sounded so strange to his ears.

"You try me sorely, lad. I would not have indulged you this long if I were not so beholden to you. Now speak, or the bear will be killed and the matter will be ended."

Wat believed the King meant his threat. "Yes, I will try," he answered. "What island? How can we go to it?"

The King waved. "It is an island where we keep our horses grazing. We will send you on the ship that brings them to the mainland. Some will remain, so do not let the bear kill them. There are sheep that can be eaten, but I hope the bear will catch fish and seals for its food. We will leave you provided with a portion of barley, and there are shepherds' huts for shelter. There is no wood. You must burn the turf. You will learn about that. Will you mind being so alone?"

Wat shook his head.

"And then, when I have dealt with the Lord of Urris and my kingdom is in order and the court settled, I will send for you and the bear. If you persuade the girl to stay with you, she may come, too. If she desires to return to her homeland, she will be sent to Firland, which is partway to the Land of the White Falcons." He smiled again. "Shall you have it in writing?"

Wat could tell that the King was mocking him, but not with ill humor. Returning the smile, Wat said, "Not unless it is writ in the bear speech."

The King threw back his head with a laugh. "It is settled, then." He clapped a rough hand on Wat's shoulder. "Now you must be gone from here while I find someone to make ready for the bear. I would have you on your way with the next ebb tide."

Wat ran out to the courtyard. He followed the delicious aroma of bread to a cooking hut, but the baker had no ready loaves yet and could only nod Wat toward the honey pot. Wat dipped his hand inside and sucked the golden sweetness from his fingers. "Where is the King's bread?" he asked, seeing no wheaten flour.

The baker swept a doughy hand over the board. "There are no royal bakers or cooks here, for the finery of his household would give away his presence. Since we landed on this coast, we have lived simply. Only barley grows on the scant plowlands. Come back in a while and you shall taste the King's loaf. Or," he added with a laugh, "one like it."

Wat went on around to the rear of the hall and climbed the steps to the stone platform. Now that the wind had dropped, he could hear the waves more distinctly. It was dizzying to look straight down where the sea splintered against the wall.

Kaila was still there, though farther off. Yet she could see the guards on the platform. She must have guessed that Wat was in the fortress. It probably never occurred to her that he might not come. He felt a flicker of irritation at her certainty. He suspected that when he told her of the bargain he had struck with the King of Thyrne, she would be unimpressed. No doubt she would shrug and wonder why he had not handled it some other, better way.

Suddenly he leaned out and shouted her name. She was looking seaward, scanning the water, her hands shielding her eyes. "I'm coming!" he shouted hoarsely, but his words were like grains of sand in the expanse between them. Of course, she knew he was coming. That was why she was waiting for him.

Maybe it was just as well that his voice could not reach her. He couldn't persuade her of the King's claim on them, not all at once. On the island there would be time to sort out what they had lost and what they had gained, time to explore the other kind of freedom Gunni had spoken of, the kind that cannot be bought with a bride price. If Kaila's rules, the different rules she lived by, were part of the bear lore he had set himself to learn, the lessons might be a kind of rehearsal. To play a part, Dodder had instructed over and over again, you must be willing to be changed. To pretend is to become. On the island they would live as though they were free.

Some distance out, the bear surfaced, her forepaws paddling hard, her hind legs straight behind. She dived and reappeared with a fish in her mouth. Splashing through the breakers, she stopped midway between Kaila and the fortress. She bit into the fish, then shook herself, sending a shower of dazzling droplets into the air.

"Fish!" Wat yelled down to her. "Fish!"

The bear looked all around for him. Then, with her prey clamped firmly between her jaws, she galloped down the beach to share it with Kaila.

Raw fish, thought Wat. Kaila was welcome to it. On the island they would cook what they caught on a turf fire. He stood watching Kaila and the bear tearing at the fish. Then he climbed down from the wall and went back to see if the barley bread was out of the oven. It was likely to be the last he would taste for some time to come.